# MY DEAREST HOLMES

# *My Dearest Holmes*

## *A recently discovered memoir by John H. Watson, M.D.*

*Edited by Rohase Piercy*

First published in 1988 by GMP Publishers Ltd
PO Box 247, London N15 6RW, England
Distributed in North America by Alyson Publications Inc.,
40 Plympton St, Boston, MA 02118, USA


**British Library Cataloguing in Publication Data**

Piercy, Rohase
My dearest Holmes.
I. Title
823'.914[F]

ISBN 0-85449-081-7

Cover illustration by Sidney Paget, originally
published in *The Strand* magazine.

Printed in the European Community
by Nørhaven A/S, Viborg, Denmark

*For Jayne*
*with all that goes without saying*

The following instructions were found attached to the present manuscript; which, along with other accounts of a similar nature, have passed into my hands from a source which I am not at present at liberty to disclose.

Since they bear directly upon the circumstances under which Dr Watson wrote this account, I have reproduced them here, by way of a preface.

Rohase Piercy

It is my specific wish and intention that the manuscripts contained in this box be left unopened, unread and unpublished until one hundred years have passed since the events described in the first account (namely the year 1887).

If this length of time appears in retrospect to have been excessive, I can only apologise to the future generation. It seems to me now, in this first decade of the new century, that some further decades at least must elapse before these reminiscences can be received with such sympathy and respect as I hope will one day be possible.

The accounts of these cases have never passed through the hands of my literary agent, Dr Conan Doyle, nor do I intend that they ever shall; they are too bound up with events in my personal life which, although they may provide a plausible commentary to much of what must otherwise seem implausible in my published accounts of my dealings with Mr Sherlock Holmes, can never be made public while he or I remain alive. However, it is my hope that, when all those involved have long passed beyond all censure, these accounts may see the light of a happier day than was ever, alas, granted to us.

John H. Watson, M.D
London 1907

# *A Discreet Investigation*

## —*I*—

I HAVE OFTEN been accused of being imprecise in my datings of the many of his cases in which my friend, Mr Sherlock Holmes, allowed me to play a part; in reply I usually allude to the delicacy with which the subject matter of many of the said cases demands that they be treated.

How much more so does this apply to the present narrative!

However, it has always been possible for the discerning reader to make an accurate placing of a particular case, and since it is questionable whether this story will ever see the light of day, I see still less reason to be overly cautious; much will be explained, then, by my simply stating that the events I am about to describe took place during the January before the Sholto affair, which I have presented for public consumption under the title of 'The Sign of Four'.

Mr Sherlock Holmes had spent several days in bed, as was his habit from time to time. He was indulging in one of those periods of lassitude which frequently overtook him between cases. On this occasion, he had gone so far as to confine himself to his room, whither he had conveyed his old clay pipe, the Persian slipper containing his shag tobacco, and his cocaine bottle and hypodermic syringe; presumably he wished to avoid altogether my expressions of concern and censure on the subject of self-poisoning. I was left to console myself with the contents of the spirit flask, and to make some half-hearted attempt to restore order to the chaos of our sitting room, now that I at last had the opportunity.

I had no enthusiasm for the task, however. The melancholy which had crept up on me over the last few months seemed set to stay with me, and Holmes' withdrawal of his society served to throw my unhappy situation into even sharper relief. Forlornly I contemplated the relics of our six years' shared tenancy of the said sitting room; so much of him, it seemed, and so little of me. His books and newspapers lay in drifts in every corner. The spattered table on which his chemicals and test-tubes stood neglected would, I was sure, express feelings very similar to mine, if some miracle were to render it animate; the reference books and commonplace books on his shelf beside the fireplace, cross-indexed and kept meticulously up to date, evinced more signs of loving care than either of us; and when I found myself expressing a morbid sympathy with the sheets of unanswered correspondence firmly skewered to the mantelpiece by the wretched man's jack-knife, I decided that it was high time to abandon the whole idea of wasting any loving care on 221B Baker Street, and to seek solace elsewhere. Consequently, I absented myself from our lodgings, and spent most of my time in the environs of Piccadilly, returning in the early hours of the morning, somewhat the worse for wine.

Thus it was that I was not present when the first interview took place between Miss Anne D'Arcy and Mr Sherlock Holmes. It was over by the time I arrived back at Baker Street. I made my way unsteadily to my room, and flinging my clothes upon the floor and myself upon the bed with very little ceremony, was insensible in a matter of seconds. Due to the excessive amount of alcohol in my blood, I must have passed out rather than slept for the first few hours; and it seemed to me that it was still the middle of the night when I was dragged unwillingly into wakefulness by a tugging at my shoulder.

'Watson. Wake up.'

I gave a violent start, my eyes sprung open to the cold sunlight of a January morning. Sherlock Holmes was standing by my bed in his mouse-coloured dressing gown, his unsavoury before-breakfast pipe in his mouth. Amusement played about his lips as he surveyed me from under heavy lids, his head on one side.

'It is nine o'clock, Watson,' he said as I blinked stupidly up at him, propped upon one elbow in the bed. 'Breakfast is laid downstairs.'

It took me some time to gather my wits. I had hardly set eyes on him for days on end, much less been able to persuade him to eat with me at the proper times, and here he was, not only out of bed and ready for breakfast, but apparently anxious that I should share it with him.

'What's got into you, Holmes?' I demanded, adding somewhat peevishly, 'I'm very tired, you know. I had a late night.'

Holmes chuckled and rubbed his hands together.

'My dear fellow,' he said, taking his pipe from his mouth and surveying me with mock innocence, 'you seem to be drifting into dissolute habits. It's not like you to refuse an offer of breakfast.'

I rolled out of bed and snatched my dressing gown.

'It's not like you to exhibit such tender care over my eating habits. *You* have not been seen at breakfast for the past five days. I think I'm entitled to an explanation.'

'My dear Watson,' he said, turning to the door, 'an explanation you shall have. Over breakfast.'

Hastily I thrust my feet into my slippers and stumbled after him, knotting the cord of my dressing gown and wincing as a sudden stabbing pain attacked my temples.

'I had a visitor last night,' said Holmes as he descended the stairs ahead of me. 'If you had not been out at your club, you would have been witness to the beginnings of what promises to be rather an interesting case.'

I forebore to correct him concerning my whereabouts of the previous evening, and followed him into the living room, which had, I noted, already ceased to bear any trace of my attempts to tidy up. The breakfast table, laid with Mrs Hudson's customary primness, was as always a salutory reproach to its surroundings.

Holmes sank languidly into his armchair and watched me as I approached the table and poured us both some coffee. I noted that his face was gaunt and pallid, testifying to his unhealthy life of the last few days. I placed his cup beside the place laid for him, and drew up my own chair a little more abruptly than was necessary, causing the china to rattle. I was determined that he should at least breakfast properly before setting out on any investigation.

'Well?' I enquired tersely as I helped myself to bacon and eggs. 'Who was he? The visitor?'

Holmes smiled as he rose from the armchair and approached the table.

'She, Watson, not he,' he corrected gently. 'My client of last night was a young woman, who, if you had been here to see her, would no doubt have made a singular impression upon you.'

'No doubt,' I snapped, setting about my bacon and eggs with gusto. I was in no mood to be teased.

'A most forceful personality,' continued Holmes. 'I should imagine Miss D'Arcy can be quite formidable when she chooses to be. There was a — directness about her manner which I thought would appeal to you, Watson. Not that I can pretend to be *au fait* with your taste in ladies.'

He actually bit and chewed a piece of dry toast. I said nothing, but passed the butter dish and the marmalade.

'She left me three interesting documents which you may care to examine,' he pursued, crossing to the mantelpiece, the dry toast still in his hand. He took a small pile of papers from the shelf and put them down on the table beside my plate. He remained standing beside me, nibbling at his toast absent-mindedly. I put down my knife and picked up the yellow envelope that lay at the top of the pile. I extracted the telegram and read it while working my way through a mouthful of bacon.

It was addressed to Miss Maria Kirkpatrick, of Camberwell Grove, was postmarked Kensington and dated the 16th of January. The message was short and to the point: 'COME AT ONCE NEED HELP MOTHER', with no stops and no signature.

'I thought you said the young lady's name was Miss D'Arcy,' I said, when I had swallowed enough to make enunciation possible.

'So I did. This telegram is addressed to Miss D'Arcy's companion, with whom she lives. Upon receiving it, Miss Kirkpatrick apparently made a hasty departure from the house, and Miss D'Arcy has not seen her since.'

'Well, that is reasonable enough, surely, if her mother needs her so urgently. Has she not enquired for her at her mother's house?'

Holmes clicked his tongue impatiently.

'It is not quite as simple as that, my dear Watson. Not only has Miss D'Arcy no idea where her companion's mother lives, but she was, until the advent of this telegram, completely unaware of her existence. Miss Kirkpatrick had apparently always given the impression that her mother was dead.'

I put down the telegram and took a gulp of coffee.

'Then why did Miss D'Arcy not go to the police? Why come to you? I must say, Holmes, this sounds like an open-and-shut case of a missing person to me.'

'Patience, my dear Watson, patience. Have the goodness to examine this envelope.'

He leant over my shoulder and turned it towards my plate.

'Read it. Examine it. Let me hear what you deduce from it.'

It was addressed, like the telegram, to Miss Maria Kirkpatrick. The handwriting was large and flourishing. The envelope itself was battered and creased, as if it had been screwed up and later smoothed out again. I said as much to Holmes, who gave me a patronising murmur of assent.

'Who is this from, then?' I said impatiently. 'Miss Kirkpatrick's mother again?'

Holmes, who had sidled round the table and taken another piece of dry toast to munch upon, had his mouth full and did not reply immediately; and in the interval I was suddenly struck by the realisation that the handwriting was familiar to me. I gave an exclamation of astonishment and bent to examine the envelope more closely.

'The looped "l", the Greek "e"...' I murmured.

Holmes stepped back from the table and surveyed me in surprise, his head on one side.

'My dear boy, I begin to have hopes of you after all. As you observe, this is not a woman's handwriting; it was therefore not written by Miss Kirkpatrick's mother. And yet there is a definite link between the letter which this envelope contained and the telegram which you have just read.

'The envelope was found by our client Miss D'Arcy immediately after her companion's disappearance. She recognised it as one of a number of envelopes received by Miss Kirkpatrick from time to time, and always treated in a most secretive manner; she would never disclose the contents of these letters or the identity of her correspondent, and according to Miss D'Arcy, always destroyed both letter and envelope after reading it. This envelope, however, having been crumpled into a ball, was inadvertently laid to one side instead.'

Again I perused the bold flourishing hand, and knit my brows as I tried to remember where I could possibly have seen it before. Someone, somewhere, had written me out a name and address in just such a hand — the lines of the address on the envelope recalled it.

'According to our client,' continued Holmes, picking up a third piece of toast and putting it down again, 'Miss Kirkpatrick received this particular letter some three days before the telegram, but contrary to her usual custom she did not destroy it. Upon receiving the telegram, she apparently rushed upstairs to her room, took the letter from the envelope, glanced several times from letter to telegram, pocketed the letter, screwed up the envelope, and hurried from the house leaving the telegram and crushed envelope upon the table. This our client has gleaned from the housemaid, who was in the room at the time, and whose presence Miss Kirkpatrick overlooked in her haste and distress. We have no reason to doubt the housemaid's word; hence, my dear Watson, we may conclude that the letter and the telegram emanate from the same source. The fact that Miss Kirkpatrick did not immediately destroy this particular letter indicated it contained some important material to which she knew she might wish to refer. She had, according to Miss D'Arcy, been much preoccupied since receiving it.'

I pushed the offending envelope to the other side of my plate. 'I thought you said it was a man's handwriting and was therefore not written by Mrs Kirkpatrick,' I said casually, thinking it wiser for the moment not to reveal the familiarity of the handwriting to me, since I could not yet place it.

Holmes gave a patronising sigh.

'So I did, but that is not to say that it does not emanate from Mrs Kirkpatrick,' he said. 'I can think of a thousand explanations, the most obvious being that she had someone address her letters for her. But we must not be too hasty. It is a capital mistake to theorise before one is in full possession of the facts.'

He returned to his chair and took up his coffee, now cold. He sipped at it without appearing to notice, and watched me as I examined the final document upon the table. It was another envelope, this one containing a letter, and addressed to Miss Anne D'Arcy. It had been delivered by hand. Inside was a single sheet of paper, on which a short note was written in a firm, round hand. It was dated the 17th of January.

> My dearest A -
>
> Please do not worry about me, for I am quite safe and well, and will return home as soon as I am able.
>
> I have been called away on an urgent matter, and promise to explain all when I return.
>
> Above all, I beg you not to try and find me, and especially not to inform the police. It is a delicate matter, and you will soon know all.
>
> You must believe, my dearest, that I am safe and well, and will be with you as soon as I can.
>
> All my love,
> M.K.

'You will remark,' said Holmes, 'that the letter was written in haste, and in some agitation; see how the lady repeats herself; and the ink has been hastily blotted. Also it has been delivered by hand, to avoid a postmark; but I think we can assume that it comes from Kensington, since that is the postmark upon the telegram.'

'I see,' I said, folding the note and replacing it in its envelope. 'And Miss D'Arcy presumably does not feel satisfied to wait for her companion's return as this letter urges her to do?'

'It has been five days, with no further communication. Rather than go to the police, since Miss Kirkpatrick especially forbids it, she has approached me, to see if I can make discreet enquiries, and thereby set her mind at rest at least. She naturally finds that her dearest friend — you will gather from the note that they are on intimate terms — has kept her mother's existence a secret, and that communication with her has produced such a situation of panic, very worrying.'

'Yes, well, I can see that,' I said slowly. I was still puzzling over the handwriting. I bit into the piece of toast and marmalade I had prepared, and found it to be so cold as to be inedible. I replaced it on my plate in disgust, and looked across at Holmes, who was lying back in his chair lazily blowing smoke-rings.

'You have scarcely eaten any breakfast!' I admonished, annoyed also that he had prevented me from concentrating upon mine.

'Never mind, my dear fellow,' he replied, 'this case will do me more good than twenty breakfasts. As a medical man, you will soon see that I am right.'

I sighed, and wiped my fingers on my napkin. I realised I felt far from well, and wondered whether it had in fact been wise to tackle my bacon with such gusto.

'I am going to dress,' I announced with dignity, rising from my chair and crossing to the door.

'Yes, do, there's a good fellow,' said Holmes. 'You don't want to greet our client in your dressing gown.'

'Why,' I cried, turning back, 'when are you expecting her?'

'At any moment,' he replied, glancing at the clock upon the mantelpiece. 'We arranged that she should return here at ten.'

I raised my eyebrows. 'Then why do you not change out of your dressing gown?' I asked.

Holmes chuckled. 'I fully intend to. It will be a simple matter to remove it. Unlike you, my dear Watson, I am fully dressed beneath.'

I gained the privacy of my room as speedily as I could, and slammed the door behind me.

## — II —

IN MY HASTE to wash, dress and shave in the few minutes available, I wrenched a button from my waistcoat, broke a shoelace, and cut myself just beneath the left cheekbone. Surveying myself mournfully in the glass, I tried to create an injured, noble air; but the distinctly pink tinge to what were normally the whites of my eyes, and the shadows beneath them, made this difficult to maintain convincingly.

I had heard, in the midst of my sartorial struggles, the entry of Mrs Hudson into the room below and her subsequent retreat with the breakfast tray. Now I heard her stately tread upon the stair again, followed by lighter footsteps, and the murmur of feminine voices on the landing. Then came the expected knock upon the door, and Sherlock Holmes' languid response.

'Miss Anne D'Arcy,' announced our landlady.

'Ah, Miss D'Arcy,' I heard him say, 'so good of you to call again. Pray take a seat.'

I waited for the sound of the door closing, and for Mrs Hudson's retreating footsteps, before descending myself.

Miss Anne D'Arcy was seated in the basket chair in which Holmes always placed his visitors, a large black umbrella planted squarely at her side like a hefty spear. She was dressed in a dark tailored suit and hat, which I had to admit contrasted very well with her fair complexion and fine light eyes. I was rather startled, however, to read in those eyes a look of amused recognition, which confused me greatly, as I had no recognition of having ever seen her before.

Holmes, immaculate in his frock coat, sat in the armchair opposite.

'This is Dr Watson,' said he, 'who has been an invaluable friend and a help to me on a great many of my cases. I trust that you will have no objection to his remaining and taking part in our interview, Miss D'Arcy?'

'No objection whatever,' replied the young lady, inclining courteously in my direction. Again I caught the amused look. I was unsure what to make of it. My own observation of her, and my knowledge of her circumstances as related to me by Holmes, made me think it unlikely that her expression was intended to be flirtatious. However, I was unwilling to take any chances. I took my seat with gravity, placing myself next to Holmes, and donned as best as I could the professional, impersonal expression that I affected when engaged in my practice. Miss D'Arcy, looking properly chastened, proceeded to confirm in more detail her story of the previous night. This morning's post had brought no word from her friend, and as well as feeling naturally very worried for her, she was determined to get to the bottom of the mystery thrown up by her disappearance.

'Maria has been receiving these letters for years,' she said, 'at the average rate of one every three months or so. At first I used to tease her about them; then I became annoyed that she would not give me so much as a clue as to whom they were from. But it has remained the one point on which she has been absolutely inflexible, throughout our long acquaintance and intimacy. She simply refuses to disclose the name of her correspondent.

'As time went by, and as I observed that the letters had no adverse affect on her, beyond the secrecy which they inspired, I thought it best to let sleeping dogs lie, and ceased questioning her upon the matter. You can imagine how surprised I was, therefore, to discover that they came to all appearances only from her mother, who she had always given me to understand had died when Maria was only sixteen years of age. I can only assume now that she was lying — though why she should think it necessary to keep from me the fact that she had a mother, I just cannot imagine.'

Here she paused with a sigh, and remained for some time gazing pensively at the Persian slipper which Holmes had restored to its place by the fire, as if trying to evince some clue from it as to her friend's behaviour.

The silence was broken by Holmes, who, leaning forward with every appearance of interest, enquired, 'How long have you known Miss Kirkpatrick, Miss D'Arcy?'

'All in all, for nearly eight years.'

'And for how much of that time would you say that you have been on intimate terms?'

Miss D'Arcy raised an amused eyebrow.

'We have shared a house for the last six years.'

'On intimate terms?'

'Yes, Mr Holmes.'

I saw that my friend had no idea of the dangerous waters into which he was drifting.

'And you never had occasion, during those six years, to meet members of Miss Kirkpatrick's family?'

'Never. Her mother, as I said, I had always assumed to be dead, and her father, I understand, lives in retirement in Sussex, where he is cared for by her elder sister, his second wife having died. At least, that is what I always understood; now I do not know what to believe! She also has a married brother. I am not sure where he lives. None of the family would welcome my acquaintance, and I do not know whether they even know of my existence.'

Holmes rested his chin upon his hands, and raised his eyebrows.

'Indeed. Why is that?'

I raised my eyes to the ceiling and amused myself by counting the cobwebs overlooked by Mrs Hudson during her weekly inspection of the rooms.

Miss D'Arcy paused before answering. I must say I thought she handled it very well.

'I assume,' she said cautiously, 'that my circumstances — that is to say, my background — my family background, the relative poverty of my childhood and upbringing, would cause some embarrassment and disapproval. The Kirkpatricks were apparently one of the foremost Sussex families, and laid great store by their social position.'

Brilliant. I almost uttered the ejaculation. By some instinct, she had touched on just the subject to inspire my friend's socialist tendencies. He loathed every form of Society with his whole Bohemian soul.

'My dear Miss D'Arcy,' he murmured, 'I am so sorry. I did not mean to cause you the slightest embarrassment. I trust you have never allowed the attitude of such ignorant people to distress you in the slightest.'

'Oh no, Mr Holmes, I can never afford to take account of the attitudes of ignorant people.'

I smiled to myself, and, looking up, was somewhat embarrassed to catch a look of annoyance from Miss D'Arcy. A slight flush rested on her cheeks. I wished that I could find some opportunity to explain myself to her; but this was hardly the time or place.

'You say that your companion usually destroyed these letters from her mother,' Holmes said. 'Did you observe her do so?'

'No, she would not have wanted to provoke my curiosity by destroying them in front of me. But I would find the ashes in the grate, sometimes with a piece of the envelope unburned, but always with the letter itself completely destroyed.'

'So that whereas she allowed herself sometimes to be careless about the envelope, she was always most careful to destroy its contents completely.'

'Exactly.'

Holmes thought for a moment, and then asked, 'How many servants do you keep, Miss D'Arcy?'

'Two men, a cook and a housemaid. They have all been with us for a considerable time, and I would certainly say that each one was to be trusted absolutely. Unfortunately, one of our men, John, is leaving us in the near future to take a situation in the country, nearer his ailing mother. We will miss him greatly.'

'You do not think that Miss Kirkpatrick would have entrusted her secret correspondence to one of the servants, unknown to yourself? She must have replied to these letters.'

Miss D'Arcy appeared to be amused by this suggestion, but she gave it several moments' thought. At length she said, 'I do not know. It would be very strange if she did...I have already asked them all if they know of any clue as to where she may have gone, and they all appear to be as much in the dark as I am. The housemaid told me of her taking the letter with her. I really don't see how I can do otherwise than take their word in the matter.'

'Hmm.' Holmes appeared to accept this, for after drumming his fingertips together for a while, he launched out on another track.

'Presumably Miss Kirkpatrick did not burn her ordinary correspondence; where does she keep her letters and papers?'

'In her desk, in her room.'

'Is the desk locked?'

'Yes. But I know where she keeps the key. She did not take it with her, and I have already searched the desk. I found nothing of any importance — that is, nothing that could have any bearing upon this present matter.'

Holmes narrowed his eyes.

'What did you find, Miss D'Arcy?'

Our client shrugged.

'My own letters to her from years ago. Photographs...several, of her brother, I presume. I had no idea that she kept his picture. Some official documents, records of financial transactions...I must confess, I did not peruse them too closely.'

Holmes was silent for a moment, then rose quickly and reached for his pipe.

'You don't mind my smoking, Miss D'Arcy,' he informed her, as he lit it.

'Not at all,' she agreed. (At least, I noticed, it was the briar, not the old clay.)

Relaxing back in his chair, Holmes exhaled several clouds of acrid smoke before remarking casually, 'These photographs of Miss Kirkpatrick's brother. You express surprise over them.'

'I must confess that I was surprised. Since I have known Maria, she has not been on speaking terms with her brother, on her own account as well as on mine. They never even exchange Christmas greetings.'

Holmes' exhalations grew more copious. 'You have never met this brother,' he said at length, removing the pipe from his mouth, 'and yet you obviously recognise his photograph. Had Miss Kirkpatrick shown you his photograph before?'

Miss D'Arcy widened her eyes in surprise. 'Why, no. But I naturally assumed that it was he. He looks so like her...in his eyes, the shape of his face...his hair is lighter, though. He is very young, in the photographs. In his early twenties, I mean. They must date from a time before there was bad feeling between them. He must be well on in his forties by now. He looks very...different from the way I imagined him, I must say.'

'I see. And are all these photographs of the same age?'

'No, there are two or three of him as a young boy.'

'Indeed? That is most surprising.'

'Is it, Mr Holmes?'

'You do not think so?'

'Well...if she has kept these early photographs I see no reason why she should not also have kept some childhood ones.'

Holmes regarded her demurely from beneath lowered lids.

'You are not thinking, Miss D'Arcy. Would you think me very rude if I were to enquire as to your age?'

'I am twenty-nine years old.'

'Ah. But Miss Kirkpatrick is older than you, is she not? In her early forties, perhaps?'

'Yes, that is true, Mr Holmes. But how did you..?'

'Never mind, Miss D'Arcy. Now. You must do as I say. Go home, and search that desk again. You have missed something. Somewhere, among those official documents, you will find a certain paper that will reveal all. If it is not among the papers, it will be hidden somewhere in the desk. There may be a concealed drawer. There. You may take Dr Watson with you. He knows my methods, and will be able to help you. When you have found what you are looking for, return here at once. Wait for me if I am not at home. I have a few enquiries of my own to make.'

He rose as he spoke, and made as if to turn towards his room. Miss

D'Arcy rose also.

'Just a moment, Holmes,' I said, scrambling to my feet in their wake, 'I want a word with you. Miss D'Arcy, if you would be so good as to wait here, I will not keep you a minute.'

I followed him into his room, which I found in a remarkable state of dishevelment. A discarded syringe lay upon his dressing table, beside its morocco case. I regarded it with a look of pointed disapproval, which produced no response from Holmes except a soft chuckle. He sat upon the edge of the bed, rubbing his hands together and regarding me with amusement.

'Well, Watson? Yes, you see that I have been indulging in self-induced lethargy. But this case has brought me out of it, so your censure would be a little too late. Now, what is the problem?'

'Well,' I said confusedly, 'I just thought you might give me some more information. You appear to be sending me off to search for a missing document. Might I be permitted to know the nature of the said document, for instance?'

'My dear Watson,' he said, 'you may not. If you cannot deduce it, you do not deserve to know.'

'But damn it all, Holmes, how am I to deduce it from the fact that the lady keeps photographs of her brother? You know that you work too fast for me. Look here, I'm always willing to be of service, and you send me off on the most absurd wild goose chases. You're always taking advantage of me when I'm in the dark.'

'No I'm not, my dear fellow,' said Holmes soothingly, 'not really.'

I sighed heavily. He affected not to hear.

'Now, how am I taking advantage of you,' he continued reasonably, 'in sending you off in the company of an attractive young woman to make a simple search of a lady's writing desk? Your powers of observation are as good as mine. I simply want you to bring back to me the rather startling document which I deduce you will find there. You will know what it is when you see it, so what is the point of my telling you in advance? But look now. The clue is in the telegram. What did the telegram say?'

'Come at once need help mother,' I repeated.

'There now,' said Sherlock Holmes triumphantly.

I was still in the dark, and he knew it; but I was not going to give him the pleasure of teasing me further. I sniffed in an aggrieved manner, and turned to the door.

'Very well, Holmes,' I said with dignity, 'I will see you later.'

'You will indeed, my dear fellow,' he said, coming up unexpectedly behind me and pinching me on the arm. 'Now off you go. Our client is waiting. I'm sure she will find you much better company than me. The fair sex is your department, after all.'

Not wishing to expose my burning cheeks to his observation, I opened the door without looking back, and entering the sitting room, closed it behind me.

'Let us go, Miss D'Arcy,' I said rather curtly to our client, who stood tapping her foot impatiently by the fireplace.

## — *III* —

I HAD INTENDED to give my ruffled feelings the satisfaction of maintaining a dignified silence en route to Camberwell, but my companion had other ideas. She hailed a hansom before I had a chance to do so, gave instructions to the driver, and almost before I had settled myself properly beside her, she thumped briskly on the ceiling with her umbrella and we were off at quite an alarming pace.

I was still attempting to settle myself on the hard seat when she turned to survey me with a knowing look.

'Tell me, Dr Watson,' she said, 'is Mr Holmes really as obtuse as he pretends to be?'

I was extremely startled, and remained for some moments with my mouth open foolishly. Composure and caution, I thought as I recovered myself. That was the only approach.

'I have no idea what you mean, Miss D'Arcy,' I said haughtily.

She smiled. 'You don't recognise me, do you Dr Watson?' she said in a low voice.

My haughty manner vanished in astonishment.

'My dear madam,' I expostulated, completely out of my depth, 'I have never set eyes on you before this morning, I am sure of it.'

Miss D'Arcy appeared to inspect the handle of her umbrella. 'No? Well, that does not say much for your powers of observation, considering that I set eyes upon *you* only yesterday evening.'

Once again my mouth fell open. Composure and caution took flight. A guilty flush stole to my cheeks, as she continued calmly:

'After my visit to your lodgings last night, and my initial interview with your esteemed companion, I decided, since I dreaded returning once more to an empty house, to make one more brief search for mine. It was still reasonably early, and I did not consider that I was taking a great risk, even in making my way to some of the — less public quarters, shall we say. My intention was to seek out certain discreet meeting places which Maria and I used to visit occasionally, and make further enquiries for her there. Gossip travels fast, and one meets people from all quarters of London — at Mr Richardson's establishment, for example. But there, Dr Watson, I am telling you what you already know. For it was there I saw you, in the company, if I am not mistaken, of a promising young member of Her Majesty's Government. Of course, I did not know it was you. I simply registered the fact that I recognised your face, having seen you in similar surroundings before, from time to time.

'Imagine my surprise, therefore, when you walked into Mr Holmes' sitting room just now, and I heard you introduced as the celebrated Dr Watson, chronicler of that gentleman's notable success with the Jefferson Hope affair! I must say that I read your account of that case with the greatest interest, Dr Watson; it has made me quite an admirer of Mr Holmes, as you may gather from my coming to consult him on so personal a matter. I have heard also, of course, of his many other successes; might we hope to see some of those in print one day also? Such an accomplished narrator as yourself should not leave his talent to lie fallow for too long.'

I spent some minutes in regaining my composure, clearing my throat and moistening my lips, before I was able to favour her with a weak smile.

'Please do understand, Dr Watson,' she said, observing my confusion, 'that I mean you to take nothing I have said in the negative sense. Quite the contrary, I do assure you.'

'That's very kind of you, Miss D'Arcy, I'm sure,' I responded nervously. I saw that she read me too well to leave me any other option but to trust her. 'Well, we obviously understand one another,' I continued in warmer tones. 'But as for your question regarding Mr Sherlock Holmes, I am afraid that his attitude is not so much one of obtuseness as of complete unconcern. At least, that is how I read it. He does not...know certain things about my private life, Miss D'Arcy. Although we have shared lodgings for seven years, we are not — on intimate terms.'

I spoke earnestly, for I certainly could not afford to have her misunderstand the situation. She regarded me seriously.

'You are very fond of him, however, and would wish things otherwise,' she said.

I gripped the edge of my seat and did not reply. Turning to look at the street, I observed that we were just passing the door of the Cafe Royal and were approaching Regent Circus. I shifted my gaze abruptly to the swaying interior of the hansom. I felt Miss D'Arcy's eyes upon me.

'Is it so very obvious?' I said at last.

'Only to one with eyes to see and wit to guess. I suppose we may take this to be the one situation in which Mr Sherlock Holmes has neither.'

I sighed again and shifted my position upon the hard seat. A wave of emotion swept over me, and I could not trust myself to speak.

'I am sorry, Dr Watson,' said Miss D'Arcy quietly, 'you must forgive me. I merely wanted to satisfy my curiosity as to the nature of your relationship with Mr Holmes — a rather vulgar curiosity, I dare say, but I felt that I had laid myself open, and received no support from you in the face of his deliberate or naif failure to grasp my situation. I do apologise.'

I turned to look at her, and managed a rueful smile. 'No need to apologise, Miss D'Arcy,' I said. 'The whole situation is most unsatisfactory and ill-defined, as you have had opportunity to observe. Heaven knows where it will all end.'

We jolted along in silence for some time. As we crossed the bridge at Westminster, I thought fleetingly and reluctantly of my companion of last night, with whom Miss D'Arcy had observed me. A wave of disgust and despair swept over me, and I stared at the murky waters as we passed over to the Surrey side. It was as though Miss D'Arcy could read my mind, for she leaned towards me and spoke sympathetically.

'Mr Holmes prefers to remain enigmatic, and therefore in control,' she said. 'That at least is obvious. However, you may rest assured, Dr Watson, that he would be lost without you. Mark my words, he feels more than he shows. Perhaps one day he will feel able to say so.'

'He has never expressed affection for me,' I said in a low voice. 'Even though he can be playful, almost flirtatious at times. His sudden changes of mood used to fascinate me, at first. I had never met anyone like him. Then gradually I understood that my fascination with him was becoming too strong for comfort.'

I realised that I was about to unburden myself completely to someone whose acquaintance I had made only a couple of hours previously. I hesitated, but then reflected that she already knew so much; the damage, if damage it were, had been done. It was with a sense of relief that I continued:

'I am a medical man, as you know. It did not take me long to understand. I was not even particularly surprised; looking back, I realise that I had always known. It was ironic, really. Somehow I had gained the reputation of being quite a ladies' man. Only Holmes did not believe it. I shall never forget the look he gave me, once in the early days of our acquaintance, when I was — well, talking foolishly, exaggerating. It was cool, appraising, as if he could see right through me. I was angry then. He was amused at my anger. He still makes jokes about my prowess with the ladies.

'It may be true, as you say, that he feels more for me than he shows. But it is against his nature to express his emotions. And any display of emotion or affection towards himself would disgust him. He defends himself against anything of the sort. I do not know why. He finds life difficult, I think. Without his obsession, his cases, he would be lost. But even if he could bring himself to admit the possibility of anything between us, he would never — it would not be possible for him. And there is his reputation, and mine. I place my own at risk, I know, by the company I keep; but I have to find solace somewhere. I am no weaker in that respect than most of my sex, I believe. But I need hardly say that it is not — what I would choose.'

I lapsed into silence, and turned once more to look out at the street. We were fast approaching Camberwell. Beside me, Miss D'Arcy sighed.

'I am so sorry, Dr Watson,' she repeated. 'What can I say? I can only advise you that there *is* a need for discretion. Your reputation is, as you say, of the utmost imnportance, and in today's climate — but in any case' (here she gave a short laugh) 'there are always ways to protect oneself. As you must know, some of the most exalted figures of our society are discreetly known to be discreetly *so*. And some of my best friends have been respectable married women.'

'Indeed?' I murmured, naively shocked, though I suppose I should not have been. 'You have been most kind and sympathetic, Miss D'Arcy, and we will soon have wasted the entire journey talking about my affairs, when your own are so pressing. It is unpardonably selfish of me.'

'Not at all, Dr Watson,' she replied. 'Pray think nothing of it...It has served to divert my mind from my own troubles, and since they are in such a seemingly impenetrable muddle, the diversion has been very welcome.'

We had just turned off from Camberwell Green, and it was not long before the hansom slowed to a halt outside a large and gracious Georgian residence with a white porch. We alighted and I paid the driver while Miss D'Arcy made her way swiftly up the drive to the front door. Before she reached it, it was flung open by a distraught-looking maid, who rushed out almost into Miss D'Arcy's arms.

'Oh miss — oh miss!' she sobbed, in great emotion.

'Why, Hetty,' said my companion, obviously struggling to maintain a calmness of tone, 'what is it? Good or bad, Hetty?'

'Bad, miss,' gasped the girl; then, seeing her mistress' white face, caught at her arm, adding, 'Oh, but not as bad as that, miss. But there's been a burglary.'

'A burglary?' cried Miss D'Arcy and I together.

'Yes, miss; someone got into the upstairs rooms, this morning, while I was downstairs polishing the back parlour. I heard someone walking about overhead, in Miss Maria's room. I thought it was her come back, and I flew up the stairs two at a time, and there was this gentleman standing there behind her writing desk!'

'Good heavens,' murmured Miss D'Arcy as we followed the excited girl into the hall. She motioned us both into a room on the right. 'Let us sit down in here, Hetty, and get your breath before you continue. Dr Watson, do take a seat.'

She motioned me to a comfortable armchair and I seated myself, noting with approval the tasteful furnishing and uncluttered appearance of the room.

'Now, Hetty,' said Miss D'Arcy, 'sit here on the sofa and tell us what happened next.'

'Well, miss,' said Hetty, perching herself uncomfortably on the very edge of the sofa. 'He heard me coming, of course, and as I reached the door he turned round. When I saw his face — oh, it was such a shock, miss!'

She opened her small pale eyes to their roundest, and placed her hand upon her heart, as though reliving the moment.

'Why, Hetty, what was so shocking about him?' asked Miss D'Arcy patiently.

'Well, he was the very image of Miss Maria! Except for his hair, miss, and his clothes, of course. I was struck dumb at the sight of him, I couldn't think what to say. But he said, "Ah, you must be Hetty." Now how could he have known my name, miss? I've never set eyes on him in my life before, I swear it.'

The girl looked from her mistress to me with such a bewildered earnestness that her eyes seemed about to pop out of her head. Miss

D'Arcy looked at me in equal amazement.

'Was he a young, or an older man?' she asked.

'Young, miss. I called for John as loudly as I could,' continued the girl, 'and the gentleman began to move backwards towards the window, saying, "Now, Hetty, don't. There's no need to be afraid." But when he heard John come running up the stairs, he was off out the window as quick as anything. John and I both looked out after him and saw him running across the garden and over the hedge. John ran down to catch him, but he had got clean away by then.'

Miss D'Arcy stood up and half turned to the window, as though to catch a glimpse of the fleeing burglar.

'Did he take anything from the desk?' she asked.

'Don't think so, unless he'd already put it in his pocket. I don't know that he even got to open it, miss. Do you think we should call the police?'

Miss D'Arcy looked questioningly at me.

'I think we should have a look for ourselves first,' I said, 'and then contact Sherlock Holmes. He will know the best stage at which to involve the police.'

And so we made our way upstairs, stopping only to question John, the footman, a neat and dapper man, who confirmed the truth of Hetty's account.

Miss Kirkpatrick's room was light and spacious, overlooking a well-kept garden at the back of the house. The large sash windows gave a view of the garden, with a side passage leading out at the right, shielded by a hedge.

'Is this where the man got away?' I enquired of John, who had followed us into the room at our request.

'Yes, sir. Jumped over the hedge and off down the passage. I rushed downstairs to the front door, but he was off up the road, with a good start on me.'

I turned to Hetty, who stood small and apprehensive in the doorway. 'And the window was open, was it Hetty, when you came into the room and found the man?'

'Yes, sir. I don't know how he would have got in through anywhere else, sir.'

'Thank you, Hetty.'

I must admit that I always enjoyed the chance to do a little questioning and deducing for myself. It gave me a sense of importance, which was always denied me when Holmes took the centre stage. I decided to make the most of it, and debated in my mind whether he would have turned his attention first to the desk, or to the window sill. I decided upon the former; having dismissed the servants, Miss D'Arcy was already standing at the open desk, sorting rapidly through its contents.

'Is anything missing?' I enquired as I joined her.

'No; at least, I think not. Here are my letters, you see, tied together, undisturbed' — she swiftly put aside a small bundle tied with pink ribbon — 'And here are several bills, all paid; some dressmaker's receipts; Maria's appointment book — I have already looked through it, Dr Watson, it is not in the nature of a journal, and it contains no reference to any appointments or events which were unknown to me. This is her stationery; pens and blotting paper; some stamps — ah, and the photographs in which Mr Holmes showed so much interest. I think they are all here...yes. Five of them. Three of her brother as a young man, two of him as a child.'

I took and examined them. The childhood pictures were on top, and showed a somewhat excessively pretty little boy, with blond curls and a sulky expression.

'These are surprisingly good quality photographs,' I remarked, 'to have been taken — what? — forty-odd years ago? Why, the science of photography was still in its infancy!'

Miss D'Arcy took first one and then the other. 'That is true,' she said. 'I must confess I did not examine them closely before. They are all very well preserved...Why, Dr Watson, whatever is the matter?'

She had heard me give a gasp. I was looking at the later photographs, which showed a young man who still retained his childhood beauty, though the petulant air was replaced by a somewhat dandified and dissolute one. The thick wavy hair, the small mouth, the cool light eyes with their long lashes, were quite familiar to me.

'But...I know this man,' I faltered.

Miss D'Arcy looked at me sharply. 'You? But how could you know Maria's brother? Besides, he is much older now than when those pictures were taken. You must be mistaken.'

'No,' I insisted, turning to her slowly, 'I am sure I am not. These pictures, in my opinion, were taken quite recently. They cannot be of Miss Kirkpatrick's brother, though they may be of some younger relation, for he certainly shares her name. This is undoubtedly my friend, Maurice Kirkpatrick. I would not mistake him anywhere. I have often laid a bet on the horses with him, frequently to my cost. Really, it is he, I do assure you, Miss D'Arcy.'

Miss D'Arcy raised her eyes from the photograph and looked long and hard at me. I returned her stare. Then, at almost the same moment, we darted to the door and shouted at the tops of our voices for the housemaid. Our united cry brought poor Hetty scampering to the top of the stairs.

'Yes, miss?' she gasped.

'Hetty,' said Miss D'Arcy, taking the girl by the arm and drawing her to examine the photograph she had taken from me, 'Hetty, was this the gentleman you saw at Maria's desk?'

Hetty's eyes widened as she looked at the picture. 'Yes, miss, that's him,' she said at once. 'Why, I told you he looked like Miss Maria, didn't I? Who is he, then?'

'I'm afraid I don't know, Hetty,' said Miss D'Arcy, gently releasing her. 'But I intend to find out.'

She walked slowly back into the room, leaving the astonished girl on the landing. Quietly I dismissed her, and followed Miss D'Arcy.

'I think,' I said, as I watched her mechanically removing the remaining contents from the desk, 'in fact, I *know* that I have Kirkpatrick's address somewhere. He wrote it down for me, having lost his card. I knew I recognised that handwriting from somewhere.'

'What handwriting, Dr Watson?' she asked absently.

'Why, the handwriting on the envel — ' I stopped in mid-word, and she stopped in mid-action. Once again, we stared at one other.

'Those letters,' I said at last, stating the obvious,'they are from him.'

Miss D'Arcy deposited the last of the desk's contents upon the chair. 'But who..?' she ventured softly. 'Who is he? A cousin? A nephew? But she said that her sister was unmarried, and her brother childless...'

She was prevaricating and we both knew it.

'Holmes was suspicious of these photographs even from your description of them,' I said gently. 'He was ahead of us in this. He said to me that the clue was in the telegram.'

'The telegram,' repeated Miss D'Arcy reluctantly.

'COME AT ONCE NEED HELP MOTHER.'

There was no need for either of us to quote it.

I crossed over to the desk. 'I think,' I said calmly, 'that at last I know what we are looking for.'

She rallied herself. 'And so do I. But where? The desk is empty. You have seen all the papers.'

'A secret compartment, then. There must be one, as Holmes said.'

I stood back to let Miss D'Arcy's nimble fingers search the

interior of the desk. It was small enough, and simply made, but her fingers paused as she tapped at the back panel.

'It is here,' she said, 'I am sure of it. It has a hollow sound. Listen.'

I listened, and then, motioning her aside, inspected the back panel myself for a spring or a catch. There was none. Meanwhile Miss D'Arcy, who had moved round to the back of the desk, was searching from the other side. At once, she gave a cry of satisfaction.

'Here! Look, Dr Watson. There is a spring at the side, at the corner. This must be it. Now we have only to find out how to — '

Even as she spoke, the back panel shot out at her touch upon the spring, so that it protruded sideways from the desk. With a startled exclamation, Miss D'Arcy fumbled behind it and withdrew a small piece of paper, neatly folded. She opened it with trembling fingers, looked at it for a moment, then handed it to me.

It was, as we had expected, the certificate of Maurice Kirkpatrick's birth. His mother was named — the surname her maiden name, Kirkpatrick, the Christian names Maria Constance Louise. The space for entry of the father's name and occupation had been left blank.

I am afraid that my first reaction was one of embarrassment for my friend. I was ashamed of having inadvertently discovered his origins in this manner, and a guilty blush stole to my face. When I looked across at Miss D'Arcy, however, I quickly recovered myself. She had sunk into the chair, white to the lips.

'My dear Miss D'Arcy,' I cried, rushing to her. 'Pray do not take it so hard. Sit back now, there. Let me get you some brandy.'

I ran to the door and shouted for some brandy, which the footman brought. In answer to his anxious enquiry, I dismissed him hurriedly with orders to get a cab as quickly as possible.

I held the glass to Miss D'Arcy's lips, and it seemed to revive her a little. I took her hand, which was cold as ice, and tried to chafe some warmth back into it.

'Please, my dear Miss D'Arcy,' I said, 'please, I beg of you, take a hold of yourself. All will be explained, I promise you. It cannot be quite as bad as you think. I am sure she did not mean deliberately to deceive you, but only to spare you pain. You must believe it.

'There,' I continued as I saw the colour begin to steal back into her cheeks, 'take another sip. That is better. Now, listen. I have ordered a cab. We must return to Baker Street at once. If anyone can sort out this tangle with the greatest discretion in the shortest time, it is Sherlock Holmes.'

Our journey back to Baker Street was certainly in contrast to our drive to Camberwell Grove, for we sat in absolute silence, each occupied with our own musings. Two thoughts occurred to me in quick succession; the first irrelevant at this stage, the other ignoble under the circumstances:

I had forgotten to make an examination of the window sill, to ascertain how Kirkpatrick had reached the first floor room; and I was going to have to expose my acquaintance with that gentleman to the searching questions of Sherlock Holmes.

## — *IV* —

WE FOUND Mr Sherlock Holmes busily engaged in cross-indexing his reference book, a pile of newspapers on the floor beside him. He looked up when we entered, a smile of satisfaction playing across his ascetic features.

'Ah,' he said as Miss D'Arcy handed him the certificate. 'So it did not take you long to find it. It is just as I expected. I have taken the precaution of ascertaining the young gentleman's address — I have not been idle in your absence, you see; Kensington is not overpopulated with young Mr Kirkpatricks — so we can move on quickly to the next stage of our investigation.'

'The gentleman in question nearly beat us to the goal,' I said. 'He apparently tried to burgle Miss D'Arcy's house this morning, and I presume it was this certificate that he was after.'

It always gave me the greatest pleasure to be able to surprise Holmes. For a moment he regarded me with a look of pure astonishment. Then he chuckled, and rubbed his hands together.

'Dear me,' he said, 'this case gets more and more intriguing! Pray take a seat, Miss D'Arcy — I do beg your pardon. Now, suppose you let me have the story of this interesting burglary.'

He listened in silence as Miss D'Arcy told him of the morning's discovery. He had completely recovered his composure, and his heavily-lidded countenance betrayed nothing of the excitement of which I knew this expression to be a sign. The smoke curled quickly from his pipe and hung in the air between us and him. Not even at the mention of my acquaintance with Miss Kirkpatrick's son did he display the least sign of outward interest.

'Well, well,' he murmured when Miss D'Arcy had finished. 'This really is a very interesting development. I must admit, I had not anticipated this. This certificate, the existence of a son, yes — but that he should take the risk of breaking into his mother's house in broad daylight, not knowing, Miss D'Arcy, that you were not at home...He was looking presumably for this certificate, as you say — I think, by the way, that it would be safest if I kept hold of it for the moment. Presumably also, he undertook this search with his mother's consent. He was standing *behind* the desk, you say; it sounds as though he knew exactly where to look. If he had not been disturbed at that precise moment, he would have taken what he came for and been off out of the window with no one any the wiser.

'Well, we have been lucky, and he unlucky this morning. Now, the question is, why was this certificate needed so urgently? It must have a direct bearing upon the nature of the trouble into which the said young man has fallen.'

His eyes assumed the vacant, dreamy expression which they always carried when his mind was racing.

'But why should Maria not come back herself for the certificate?' interrupted Miss D'Arcy. 'Why send her son to break into the house, when she could have walked in herself through the front door?'

'Oh, that is easily answered,' said Holmes with a dismissive wave of his pipe. 'She did not want to run the risk of encountering you, or any member of the household. There is obviously some secrecy attached to the matter, over and above the fact of her son's existence.'

Miss D'Arcy bit her lip, thought for a moment and then said in a low voice, 'Mr Holmes, I am not at all sure that I can justify asking you to continue this investigation. I can see it now in the light of an unwarranted intrusion into Maria's private affairs. If she has kept the existence of her son from me for so long, I am sure she would not want me to pry into whatever trouble has caused him to summon her to his aid like this. Perhaps it would be wisest and most honourable after all if I waited as she has asked me to do, and let her explain the matter to me in her own time.'

Holmes listened meekly enough, but his eyes, narrowing to bright slits, betrayed his desire not to abandon the chase now that he found himself to be hot on the scent. He laid his pipe aside and placed his fingertips together.

'You are my client, Miss D'Arcy,' he said, 'and it is certainly your right to forbid me from pursuing the case further if you wish. But I would urge you to think carefully before coming to that decision. Mr Kirkpatrick is obviously in some trouble, and it is by no means certain that his mother will be able to help him; whereas we, if we can discover the nature of his trouble, may be able to do just that. His rather desperate and surprising attempt at burglary this morning indicates that there is some fear that his birth certificate will fall into the wrong hands, thus escalating some form of crisis. To my mind, this points to only one possible state of affairs — blackmail.'

Miss D'Arcy seemed extremely shocked by this assertion. I was myself surprised, but being used, after so many years , to my friend's rapid trains of thought and startling deductions, I tended to underestimate the effect on the uninitiated. 'Blackmail!' she repeated, in great confusion, leaning forward in her chair and fixing her gaze on my friend's face. 'But who — why?'

'Well, Miss D'Arcy, that remains to be seen; though I think I can deduce it without too much trouble. However, I shall require proof, and I shall require authorisation from you that I continue the investigation. If you agree, Miss D'Arcy, I would advise you to remain discreet, and return home for the present, leaving the next stage to me. When I have all the information I need, I shall wire you and we can meet to discuss how best to proceed in the matter. I am sure you will agree that it is better not to involve the police at this stage.'

He had completely cast aside his languid manner, and spoke rapidly, with urgent gestures of the hands. I could tell he was anxious to be allowed to pursue the case.

Miss D'Arcy also seemed much agitated. She hesitated only fractionally before saying, 'Well, if things are really as you say, Mr Holmes, then — yes, I think you had better continue your investigations. But what do you intend to do?'

Holmes relaxed visibly. 'I intend to call on Mr Maurice Kirkpatrick,' he said airily. 'And I think — yes, I *think* I shall take Watson with me, since he is already acquainted with the gentleman.'

'But Holmes, my dear fellow,' I interjected, 'what is he going to think, if I turn up at his house with you? What excuse am I going to give? I have never visited him at his home before. He'll think the whole thing very suspicious.'

'Tut, Watson, he won't *know* that it is I,' said Holmes with a mischievous sparkle in his eye. 'You certainly didn't think I was going to introduce myself as Mr S. Holmes, consulting detective on the trail of his missing mother? No, no, my dear Watson, we are going to use a little imagination here, a little finesse. However, Miss

D'Arcy,' he continued, turning to our client, 'the best thing for you to do is, as I said, to return home. You may rest assured that I will be in touch as soon as I have proof of the matter in my hands.'

'Very well, Mr Holmes,' said Miss D'Arcy reluctantly. 'I leave the investigation with you. But do you really think that blackmail is at the root of it?'

'My dear lady, I am sure of it! What other explanation is there? Believe me, Miss D'Arcy, there is no more unscrupulous figure in our society than the blackmailer; this is why we must be on our guard, and proceed with the utmost discretion. The safety and happiness of at least two people depend upon it.'

'Three people,' said Miss D'Arcy, with a sudden bitter expression.

'Quite so. Three. Maybe four. But be patient, Miss D'Arcy. Good day to you.'

Still she hesitated, as if wishing to say something more. But after a moment she murmured, 'Good day Mr Holmes. Good day, Dr Watson, and I thank you for your kindness and your sympathy this morning,' and left the room. We heard her footsteps on the stair, and the closing of the front door.

'Well, Watson,' said Holmes, leaping to his feet the minute she had left and beginning to pace the room, rubbing his hands together gleefully, 'this is all very exciting, is it not? This case certainly exhibits some singular features. Would you not say so? I am glad, by the way, that Miss D'Arcy found you so supportive. I can always trust you to take care of that department. And now for the next stage...'

'Now look, Holmes,' I interrupted sharply, feeling that such innuendos were in very poor taste, especially under the circumstances, 'I really must set you straight on all this. The way in which Miss D'Arcy found me supportive was not at all the way you imply. Heaven knows why you insist on propounding this fantasy about my susceptibility to women; but if you cannot see that Miss D'Arcy is — well, a confirmed spinster, then your powers of perception are considerably less than they're made out to be.'

Holmes stood in front of me with his hands in his pockets, a maddening expression of pure delight upon his face.

'My poor dear boy,' said he, 'you do underestimate me, don't you? I do assure you that I have a full and accurate grasp of the situation. There is really no need for you to lecture me about it. As for your effect on the fair sex — well, my dear Watson, you surely cannot deny they seem to find you attractive. Except for Miss

D'Arcy, of course. Now, where is the inaccuracy in my stating the obvious? Hmm?'

I clenched my teeth in frustration. It was at times like this that I most regretted the exaggerated boasts with which I had for some reason felt it necessary to regale my friends at around the time of my meeting with Holmes. What could I say? That I suspected his full and accurate grasp of the situation to be the result of his morning's research, since I had seen no evidence of it earlier? I knew he would have no hesitation in calling my bluff, and in turning the situation to his own advantage.

'Anyway, Watson,' he continued, strolling jauntily around the room with an annoying spring in his step, 'since you're so anxious to set me straight on matters of which I am ignorant, perhaps you would care to give me a little resume of your acquaintance with Mr Maurice Kirkpatrick. I must say, it really is a lucky chance, your knowing him. Now, what do you think? Would he be surprised, for instance, at your turning up at his house in the company of a smart young companion, proposing an afternoon on the turf? Or would he perhaps prefer to make the acquaintance of an older gentleman of private means and aesthetic temperament? Which shall I be, Watson? In either case, I think that a certain air of decadence would fit the bill, don't you agree?'

This kind of teasing made me even more uncomfortable, being nearer the mark of accuracy. I felt my complexion change, and crossed hurriedly to the window to regain my composure.

'Tell me first,' I said, as coolly as I could, 'just why you think he is being blackmailed?'

'Oh, I don't think *he* is being blackmailed at all,' said Holmes impatiently. 'But his father undoubtedly is, and has, rather foolishly in my opinion, called on him for help.'

'His father?' I was surprised out of my confusion. 'But he has no father!'

'Tut, Watson, I'm surprised at you. And you a medical man! Everybody has a father somewhere. We may take that as a working hypothesis in at least ninety-nine point nine per cent of cases.'

'Well, good heavens, Holmes, I mean of course he has a father, but surely — do you mean that you are assuming he knows who his father is?'

'Well, I am assuming he does now. Whether he did before this present trouble, I am not yet in a position to say. But *now*, do you see — ?' he continued, deliberately adopting the patient manner with which one explains the obvious to a child or to an idiot. 'He receives a message from a gentleman who claims to be his father, and he wishes, my good Watson, to check the gentleman's credentials, so to speak. And to whom does he apply for corroboration on the subject, do you think? Hmm? Come on now, my boy, your mental powers should be able to tackle this one.'

'Oh stop it, Holmes,' I said feebly, for I could see he was already embarking upon a fit of hilarity and I had no desire to join him. 'So he contacts his mother. But I still fail to see why it has to be blackmail.'

'Why, it could be nothing else,' said Holmes, controlling himself with difficulty. 'If the man has contacted neither his son nor the mother of his son for some twenty-odd years, nothing less than the threat of discovery could lead him to do so now. You see why I did not wish to go into the matter in front of Miss D'Arcy,' he continued in a serious voice, taking me by the elbow and leading me towards the door. 'The subject would naturally be upsetting for her. We had better wait until we have cleared the whole thing up. Now, Watson, up you go and change into a waistcoat that boasts its full regimen of buttons! I would fit a new shoelace too, if I were you; we may have a little walk ahead of us. And what a careless fellow you were this morning to nick your cheek like that. I meanwhile will go and don my accoutrements, and then I think we will make our way to Kensington, with a little detour for lunch en route.'

'Might I suggest that the *older* gentleman would be a more suitable disguise, Holmes?' I said sweetly. 'Kirkpatrick has always looked upon me, I may say, rather as a paternal figure, and since I am your senior by a mere couple of years, we can hardly expect him to do less for you.'

From the mischievous glint that stole into his eyes, I realised that somewhere in my little speech I had laid myself open to his repartee. I closed the door hurriedly and made my way to my room.

## — V —

IT WAS mid-afternoon by the time we reached Mr Maurice Kirkpatrick's elegant Kensington residence. I sent in my card and we were shown into a drawing room which was decorated rather alarmingly in red and black, with white alabaster statuettes and vases in every nook and niche. I had had no idea that my friend's general air of decadence extended to his furnishings in so vulgar a manner, and noted with amusement that Holmes, abandoning his customary sartorial primness, had managed, with the aid of a loosely knotted silk necktie and several rather tasteless rings, to create just such an appearance as would blend in perfectly with Kirkpatrick's decor.

It was only a matter of minutes before the young gentleman appeared, looking surprised and harassed, although his manner was scrupulously polite as always. Holmes had chosen for some reason to adopt the pseudonym of Mr Melmond on this occasion, and I hastily introduced him as such.

'This is really very nice of you, Dr Watson,' responded poor Kirkpatrick, 'and it is always a pleasure to meet your friends. I do hope you will excuse my rather flurried appearance. My mother is staying with me at present, and she has just received some rather worrying news about a friend. Sad news, that is. Yes, the death of an old friend. I won't bore you with the details, but I do hope you won't take it amiss if our manner is a little reserved. I should like you to meet my mother, of course; you will take some tea with us?'

He spoke hurriedly and nervously, his long-lashed eyes darting from one to the other of us; though I noticed that the glances he flashed at Holmes bore a stamp of innocent appeal with which he had long ceased to favour me.

'My dear fellow,' I said in a determined voice, 'we would not dream of imposing on your hospitality at such a time. Pray do accept our apologies for this unwitting intrusion. We will call another day.'

We had both risen, and Holmes trod heavily upon my foot as he turned to admire a Greek statuette that stood upon a side table.

'Oh, a thousand apologies, Watson,' he said in a genial voice. 'How clumsy of me! Of course, my dear Mr Kirkpatrick, Dr Watson is right. We will most certainly not intrude upon you or Mrs Kirkpatrick. But my goodness, I must take this opportunity to admire such a remarkably beautiful statuette. A miniature of Michelangelo's "David", is it not? What an exquisite copy! The proportions appear to be just right.'

'Why, Mr Melmond, you must be quite a connoisseur!' cried Maurice Kirkpatrick in delight, a slow, winning smile forming on his face. 'Yes, this is but one of my little beauties, as you can see' — here he indicated the room with a sweeping gesture. 'I am a collector, you know, in a small way. I love beautiful things. You must stay and have tea with us, I simply cannot let you go now that you have been so kind as to admire my little David. What do you think of this figure of Achilles? I found it in a little shop in Museum Street, quite by accident. No, Dr Watson, I insist that you both take tea with us. It will lift my mother's spirits, I assure you. She shares my love of Greek culture, you know, Mr Melmond. She will be so pleased to meet you. Oh yes, you must certainly stay.'

He rang the bell for the servant, and ordered tea on the spot. 'And please tell Mrs Kirkpatrick that my friends would be delighted if she will join us.'

Having procured our invitation, Holmes proceeded to make his way around the room, murmuring admiringly at every fresh monstrosity, and throwing up his hands in affected delight. I comforted myself by thinking that he cut a very foolish figure in so fanciful a get-up, and by picturing to myself the reaction of Inspector Lestrade of Scotland Yard if he could see the great detective now.

Kirkpatrick eventually joined me on the sofa while Holmes seated himself gracefully in an armchair.

'But Watson here is hiding his light under a bushel!' said he with a merry laugh; it was obvious that he was greatly enjoying himself. 'If anyone has an artist's eye for beauty, Mr Kirkpatrick, it is he. As you have, no doubt, had occasion to remark. Yes, I think I can say very decidedly that my friend here has an eye for beauty.'

He was watching Kirkpatrick as he spoke; the compliment was obviously meant for him rather than for me; and so it was received, for the affected young baggage blushed and lowered his absurd lashes in a most tasteless manner.

As I bit my lip and tried to think of a suitable rejoinder, Holmes continued, 'You have been walking the garden this morning, Mr Kirkpatrick? And my goodness, if I did not perceive you to be a gentleman of civilized habits, I would say you had been — climbing a wall?'

I must say that I was pleased to see the alacrity with which the smug look vanished from my young friend's face.

'Good heavens, Mr Melmond! Why, I...yes, I believe I took a turn in the garden; but as for climbing a wall — why, what an extraordinary notion! Whatever put it into your mind?'

'My dear sir, you have forgotten to change your shoes! There is garden earth upon them, and upon the hem of your trousers — strange, for it has not been raining lately — you must have ventured into a flower bed by mistake, I imagine, or else your gardener has been careless with some loose soil. And then, there appears to be some brick dust adhering there also and, remarkably, to the knees — I trust you do not think me rude, Mr Kirkpatrick? It is just a little trick of mine, to try out my powers of observation upon a new acquaintance. I do not mean to be offensive, I assure you, quite the opposite...And then there are your shirt cuffs, and the scuffing of your shoes...But there, I see that I have embarrassed you, and that was never my intention. My dear sir, I do not wish to pry. When a young man such as yourself has his mother to stay, he has often to resort to a little — ingenuity...'

Here, mercifully, there was a knock at the door, and tea was announced. With a watery smile at Holmes, and a most suspicious glance at me, Kirkpatrick turned his attention to the deposition of the trays, and a moment later the appearance of Miss — or Mrs Kirkpatrick, for so of course we addressed her as we rose to take part in the introductions — precluded any further allusion to our host's morning adventure.

Maria Kirkpatrick was a tall and graceful woman, and one could tell that it was she who had given her son his beautiful eyes and complexion; although her hair was darker than his, with an interesting coppery tint. There were unmistakeable traces of sadness, even of fear, upon her face, but her eyes spoke of an already well-tested courage and a determined quality which had obviously stood her in good stead over the years. Both Holmes and I warmed to her, and I longed to have some quiet words with her, to reassure her as to Miss D'Arcy's state of mind and health; but this of course was impossible under the circumstances.

It was made even more impossible by Holmes suddenly switching his attention, and his charm, from the son to the mother, and striking up an easy conversation with her about the literature and culture of ancient Greece (in which she appeared to be well versed); thus leaving me prey to the whispered enquiries of my former friend, Maurice Kirkpatrick. I found his persistence very awkward.

How long had I known Mr Melmond? Where had I met him? Had he a profession, or private means? Where did he live? And by the way, how was my celebrated friend Mr Sherlock Holmes, of whom he had heard so much? Might he look forward to an introduction to that gentleman also, in the near future?

I did the best I could, and painted a very plausible picture of a decadent gentleman of dwindling income and unreliable habits, which I fancy left my enquirer rather disappointed, if no less suspicious. As for Mr Holmes, I added casually, he was at present engaged in a case which took him from London; and really he was so busy all the time, that it was very difficult to get him to pay social calls, but I would of course do my best. Maurice Kirkpatrick sipped at his tea and continued to eye me with distrust. At last I was able to turn my attention to the other half of our party, and was interested to hear that the topic had strayed somewhat nearer home.

'And so, you know the Carstairs of Sussex?' Holmes was saying, and I could tell that his interest was genuine. 'Why, what an interesting coincidence, Mrs Kirkpatrick! I knew the younger son, Mr Edward Carstairs, at college — only slightly, I may add, but I did have occasion to visit the family home. I was anxious to consult a particular old volume for my researches, and Carstairs was kind enough to let me have use of the library there. It certainly contained many fascinating first editions; I have rarely seen such a collection. However, I did not become intimate with the family. There is almost a decade between the elder and younger brother, I believe.'

'Yes, I believe so.' Miss Kirkpatrick spoke quickly, with downcast eyes, and even I could see that we were hot on the scent.

'Did you know him?' persisted Holmes. 'Rumour has it that he was somewhat dissolute as a youth. Obviously he has now settled down, and is quite a model of respectability, I believe, and happily married. I must confess myself disappointed that I never met him; he was from home on my only visit.'

'I...knew him slightly,' said Miss Kirkpatrick; and then noticing that her son and I were listening, took the opportunity to turn the conversation. 'But Maurice, why are you not entertaining Dr Watson? How very rude you must think us, Dr Watson. Allow Maurice to help you to some cake.'

A sharp look passed between mother and son, and the latter responded with alacrity. 'Yes, Dr Watson, you really must try some of this, it's excellent,' said he, attacking the unfortunate cake with the knife in such a way as to leave no doubt that there was a vicious streak in his nature.

The rest of the meal passed rather hysterically, with both mother and son conversing wildly, and sometimes simultaneously, on every topic under the sun. Holmes remained as demure as ever, with a bon mot for every occasion, but I became confused and eventually sank into silence.

# — VI —

THAT WAS *not* a successful visit,' I murmured, as we walked hurriedly away an hour or so later.

'My dear Watson, what can you mean? It was most successful. I now have all the information I need to complete my investigations.'

I sighed in exasperation, and thrust my hands further into my pockets. 'If you measure a visit by the amount of personal information you manage to squeeze out of your hosts, regardless of the amount of distress you cause or the amount of suspicion you arouse, then yes, I suppose you could call it successful,' I snapped. 'But you will excuse *me* from applying that epithet to what must certainly rank among the most embarrassing social occasions of my life. I can never enter that house again. You realise Kirkpatrick was suspicious?'

I amazed myself; I could not remember ever daring to risk Holmes' displeasure by such an outburst before. He quickened his stride in angry silence; I matched my pace with his, the adrenaline pulsing through my veins, my heart beating uncomfortably. After a while he slowed down, and began humming to himself under his breath. I stole a glance at his face and was surprised to see that his expression was perfectly mild, as though the subject had passed completely out of his mind. This defeated me; I knew that I would have to apologise, or he would simply exclude me from the rest of the investigation.

'I'm sorry, Holmes,' I said at last. 'You must forgive me; I'm overwrought. Of course you are right to put the investigation before everything.'

'You know my methods, Watson,' he said. 'I am never one to be squeamish about details; I do what is necessary. And I can assure you that I never had any intention of ingratiating myself with Mr Maurice Kirkpatrick in the first place. Any acquaintance of that sort would be detrimental to my career, to say the least.'

He gave me a sharp look. I avoided his eyes.

'As for Miss Kirkpatrick,' he continued, 'I have no wish to cause her pain, but the matter has to be cleared up as quickly as possible for her own sake; and I can assure you, that while you were gossiping with her son over tea, I picked my way through the subject of youthful connections with what I think I may claim to be a modicum of finesse, only arriving at the home territory of the

Carstairs at the very end of our conversation.'

'Yes, Holmes, I see that,' I said. I reflected miserably that the man really was as I had so often described him, a brain without a heart. I might as well cast aside any hopes, such as Miss D'Arcy had encouraged, once and for all.

He stopped abruptly at the corner of Kensington Church Street and hailed a hansom; and we soon found ourselves travelling in silence back to Baker Street.

It was already dark by the time we gained our rooms. Holmes made straight for his bookshelf and took down a copy of *Burke's Peerage*. He then filled his old clay pipe from the Persian slipper, and sat down in silence to study the book. After some minutes spent fruitlessly pacing from fireplace to window, I seated myself opposite him and lit my own pipe. My imitative gesture seemed to please him, for he looked up at me with a grunt of satisfaction, and tapped at the open page with his forefinger.

'Now we have him, Watson. Lord Robert Carstairs, of Camden Hall, Sussex. And here is the address of his London residence, in Cavendish Square. Dear me, we are almost neighbours! Date of birth, the 27th of May, 1844. So, now nearly forty-three years of age; about the same age as Miss Kirkpatrick, wouldn't you agree?'

'Wonderful, Holmes. But are you sure that it is he? There could be a hundred and one reasons for Miss Kirkpatrick's reticence when his name was mentioned, and we are taking an enormous risk if we have nothing more to go on.'

My foolish doubts restored Holmes' good humour completely, as I had known they would. He put *Burke's Peerage* to one side, leaned back in his chair, and blew a smoke-ring of satisfaction towards the ceiling.

'My dear Watson,' said he, 'we have plenty to go on, I can assure you. You surely do not suspect me of acting on nothing more than a wild guess? Let me give you a little resume of the course of my conversation with Miss Kirkaptrick, plus one or two observations which you, my dear fellow, obviously failed to register in your highly nervous state.

'We began, as you may have heard, with the topic of ancient Greece, and moved rapidly from the mainland to the islands, which we both agreed to be well worth a visit. Miss Kirkpatrick, it transpires, has been to — but I digress. It was a simple matter to lead the conversation from there to the haunts of one's childhood and youth, and the nostalgia inspired by them. Miss Kirkpatrick expressed a great love for the county of Sussex, where she had been born and brought up. She lived there, she said, until the age of twenty-two, when her father remarried; then she left the area and came to London — the implication being that she could not like her stepmother enough to live under the same roof with her. That is plausible enough, but knowing what we know, I think we can assume that there was more to it than that. If the encounter of which Maurice Kirkpatrick is the happy result happened, as it must have done, when Miss Kirkpatrick was twenty or thereabouts, the chances are that it happened in Sussex, and that her departure from the area took place soon after her son's birth.

'If Miss Kirkpatrick's former lover now finds himself in a position to be blackmailed, he must be a public figure. The Kirkpatricks, as Miss D'Arcy rightly informed us, occupy a high social position, and their daughter would have ample opportunity to make the acquaintance of the most eligible young bachelors of the county. Two or three families sprang immediately to mind; I made my way through them until I hit upon the desired reaction.

'I do have further confirmation, however. You may have possibly noticed that a copy of *The Times* lay upon the sideboard, and that it was folded open at the Court Circular. As we rose to leave, I took the opportunity to glance at it, and read that Lord Robert Carstairs is in London visiting friends at present, but that his wife Lady Sylvia Carstairs remains at home in Sussex.

'Now, this indicates a hasty visit, does it not, arranged on some pretext no doubt, but for the real purpose of making contact with his son, in an attempt to forestall or counter the activities of his blackmailer. The fact that the newspaper in the Kirkpatrick household happened to be folded back at the very page upon which Lord Carstairs' activities were detailed may be taken, under the circumstances, as an indication that that gentleman's movements are an object of some interest.

'So, my good Watson, I submit to you once again that Lord Robert Carstairs is the man.'

'Wonderful, Holmes,' I repeated with more conviction. 'Yes, of course it is all very simple and reasonable.'

Holmes gave me a sharp look. 'I often regret having to explain my deductive processes to you, Watson,' he remarked, rising from his chair, 'since your admiration is always so fleeting. Anyway — we have identified our man. Now let us see if we can do as much for his blackmailer.'

'And how are we going to achieve that, Holmes?'

'Why, by interviewing Lord Carstairs himself! I will send him a wire, telling him to expect us this evening; we do not want to have a wasted journey and find him from home. And even if his suspicious son has had the wit to forewarn him, I do not think he will refuse to see me, if only to ascertain how much I know. I shall take the opportunity to reassure him that the visit will be in the strictest confidence.

'And now, my dear Watson, no more questions. As soon as I have sent this wire, I intend to indulge myself in a little violin practice. No better way to while away the intervening hours, or to clear the mind for the next stage of our little investigation.'

Holmes was, as I have often mentioned, an amateur violinist of no mean standard, and it was usually a pleasure for me to listen to his performance. This evening, however, something in the haunting beauty of the Mendelssohn *Lieder* struck a responsive chord of such emotion within me that I was obliged to retire to my room. I do not know whether my damp eyes registered with Holmes; I caught a look from him as I rose to leave the room, and his own expression was peculiarly gentle, as sometimes happened when he was engrossed in music. His grey eyes rested upon me with a gaze that could have been either brooding or vacant. Then, with a slight shrug, he turned towards the window and continued his playing in an even more soulful vein.

Upstairs in my room, I listened to the strains from below, and wondered for the hundredth time what was to become of me. Profoundly I wished Miss D'Arcy, Miss Kirkpatrick and my friend Maurice all to the devil; between them they had contrived to bring my unhappy situation into even sharper relief. Miss D'Arcy in particular, having drawn me out about my feelings for Sherlock Holmes, had left me, it seemed, at a point of no return. What was I to do? I was in love with the man. My double life, my nocturnal visits to the clubs and meeting places where I was accustomed to seek relief, had become odious and degrading to me. A clean break seemed to be the only answer, and yet I shrank from it.

How long would it be before I betrayed myself to Holmes? Or — for in all probability he was well aware of the extent of my affection — before he himself confronted me with his cold, logical questions, his appearance of mild surprise, his 'Dear me, my dear Watson...', his careful impression of distaste for all the softer emotions, but in particular for those directed at himself? Try as I might, I could picture no happy solution to this downward spiral.

Suddenly I became aware that the music had stopped. I listened, but there was no sound from the room below. Obviously, he had laid aside his violin to concentrate once more upon the case, unhindered by my presence, uninterrupted by my inane questions, my slowness and stupidity. How else did he see me but as a foil to himself? I was a whetstone to his mind, I stimulated him. He liked to think aloud in my presence. His remarks could scarcely be said to be made to me — many of them would have been as appropriately addressed to his bedstead — but nonetheless, having formed the habit, it had become in some way helpful that I should register and interject. And yet when he wanted to move fast, when he wanted to dispense with the process of rhetorical question, suggestion from me, definitive answer from himself, he would completely ignore me, demand my silence, or contrive to remove my presence altogether.

Such were the bitter thoughts which occurred to me as I sat forlornly upon my bed, trying to picture his movements, his frenetic pacing and smoking in the room below. Then, as I realised I could hear no footstep, no creaking of the boards as was usual when he paced the floor, I pictured him instead curled up in his chair, his feet drawn up and his head resting at an angle against the chair-back, enveloped in smoke from his pipe. The thought of him sitting silently below, and me above, appeared so bleak to me that I determined to go downstairs and join him, to sit with him in silence for company's sake. After all, why punish myself more than was necessary, by depriving myself of his presence? After a few more minutes' hesitation, I made my way downstairs and entered the sitting room.

I found him lying back relaxed in his chair, the shirtsleeve of his left arm rolled back. He turned his head at my entrance, and greeted me with a slow, arrogant smile. Even before I saw the cocaine bottle and the syringe, I knew what he had been doing. A sinking sensation in my stomach caused me to halt by the door for a second; then without a word I walked across to my chair and sank into it, my elbows on my knees and my head in my hands. My reproachful attitude produced nothing beyond the humming of a few snatches of the *Lieder* he had just been playing, which soon gave way to complete silence.

Here was another aspect of Holmes which caused me continual sorrow. His addiction to the drug and the alarming swings of mood which it engendered had long been a source of anxiety to me, and in vain I had cautioned, threatened and entreated him upon the subject.

'Perhaps you are right, Watson,' he would answer mildly. 'I suppose that its influence is physically a bad one. I find it, however, so transcendingly stimulating that its second action is a matter of small moment.'

What could I do? I had not even an appropriate excuse, beyond the call of common friendship, for my concern over the matter. Why should he change his habits for my sake, if his concern for his own health was not sufficient to motivate him? How could I say to him what I longed to say: 'I love you; I cannot bear to see you harming yourself in this way'?

It was impossible; the most that I could claim was that my influence prevented his using the drug to such an excess as he might otherwise have done, had he lived alone.

Mercifully, we had not a long evening ahead of us. Dinner was brought up at seven-thirty; I ate steadily and miserably, Holmes hardly at all, as was usual when under the combined stimulation of the drug and an absorbing case. From eight-thirty to nine-thirty he sat in his chair, apparently immersed in a black-letter volume. At nine-thirty he rose abruptly, and came to stand by the chair in which I sat, also endeavouring to read.

'Well, Watson, to work! The appointed hour for our visit draws near. Would you be kind enough to ring and order a cab? Lord Carstairs, I hope, is expecting us.'

## — *VII* —

IT WAS NEARLY ten o'clock when we arrived at Lord Robert Carstairs' London residence. An immaculate butler opened the door to us, and regarded us with deep suspicion, while the footman went to present our cards.

We were shown into a luxurious but dimly lit drawing room, where a comfortable fire was burning. A tall, elegant man with fair hair, just beginning to thin, a small moustache, and a slightly dandified style of dress and manner, rose from his armchair to greet us. His movements were slow and graceful, his voice quiet, with an edge of distrust to it despite his outward politeness and calm.

'Mr Holmes, I presume?' said he, extending his hand to my companion. 'And Dr Watson,' turning to me. 'Well, it was very good of you, gentlemen, to give me advance warning of your visit; though I must confess myself still very much in the dark as to its purpose. I have heard of you of course, Mr Holmes,' he continued, as he gestured towards two empty chairs in which we seated ourselves, 'and I would be obliged if you would explain your business at once and in plain terms, and not leave me any longer in my present ignorance and anxiety as to its nature.'

Sherlock Holmes seated himself and leaned forward, chin on folded hands, his keen gaze fixed upon Lord Carstairs' face.

'To come straight to the point, then,' he said, 'you are being blackmailed, Lord Carstairs.'

The noble lord could not disguise the expression of alarm that flashed across his countenance, though he did not appear to be taken completely by surprise. He waited some seconds before replying.

'May I ask how you come to know this, Mr Holmes?'

'You do not deny it, then.'

Lord Carstairs shrugged. 'What would be the point of denying it? If you did not know it to be the case, you would not be here. Your knowledge of it worries me, however, for I have taken every step to keep the matter as quiet and discreet as possible, in order to protect the innocent. I ask you again, how do you know of this situation?'

Holmes leaned back in his chair in evident satisfaction, and placed the tips of his fingers together. Not for an instant did his keen eyes leave Lord Carstairs' face.

'You must respect the confidentiality between myself and my client, Lord Carstairs,' he said. 'I can assure you, however, that neither Miss Maria Kirkpatrick nor Mr Maurice Kirkpatrick are aware of my involvement in the matter. The object of my visit is to be of help to you; to trace the blackmailer, without involving the police, and to assist you in bringing the matter to a close without scandal or publicity, so that Miss Kirkpatrick may return to her home in safety and in peace of mind.'

Lord Carstairs remained deep in thought for a while; then raised his eyes quickly, as one who has just found the answer to a question.

'Then I think I can deduce the name of your client, Mr Holmes; and I am very sorry that the lady has become involved this far. I understood that Maria — Miss Kirkpatrick, wanted to keep the matter from her until all had been cleared up one way or the other. How much does she know?'

'Only that Miss Kirkpatrick has a son, and that he has something to do with her disappearance. That much was sure to be revealed sooner or later, Lord Carstairs, and my client is a lady of considerable determination and perspicacity, who is moreover extremely anxious over her friend's disappearance, as is only natural under the circumstances. Surely you must all of you have realised that she would make some attempt to trace her?'

Lord Carstairs gave a shrug.

'I have every reason to hold the young lady in the highest regard,' said he firmly. 'Miss Kirkpatrick's affection for her vouches that she deserves as much. I can assure you, Mr Holmes, that in contacting my son and in asking him to warn his mother of the present danger, I had no intention of causing any embarrassment or anxiety to Miss D'Arcy. I assumed, however, that Maria — that is, Miss Kirkpatrick — would take the responsibilty for any effect that current events might have in that quarter. I merely wished to put her on her guard, and to assure her that I had every intention of complying with the blackmailer's wishes, thus ensuring that no scandal ensued. I had to contact her through my son, since I did not know her address, only his. I do not know my son well, Mr Holmes — in fact, my solicitor has been my sole point of contact with him for these last fifteen years or so — but I'm afraid that he appears to be liable to panic and to overdramatise. I had not realised that he would summon Maria away from her home in such a particularly unsubtle manner. I suspect, in fact, that he is inclined to be a little jealous of his mother's affection for Miss D'Arcy.'

Holmes gave a wry smile. 'Yes, I should imagine he finds it irksome that while he is well aware of Miss D'Arcy's existence, and her importance in her mother's eyes, she remains in blissful ignorance of his. She has suffered a rude awakening on that score, however, and it will not be long before she feels ready to tackle the task of ascertaining the identity of his father. But what about yourself, Lord Carstairs? What are your feelings on the matter?'

Lord Carstairs waved his hand in a gesture of dismissive embarrassment.

'Well, well, my dear sir, it was all a long time ago, though my affection and respect for Maria Kirkpatrick has always remained. Of course, I was not jealous; I wish only for her to be happy, in her own way. She deserved to be, certainly, for she sacrificed her reputation for mine, all those years ago, without a word of reproach.'

It occurred to me that Miss Kirkpatrick's present mode of living might well in itself be construed as a reproach for her treatment at his hands. The thought must have shown in my face, for he turned to me almost with a look of appeal.

'I offered her marriage, you know; please do not think the worst of me. It was she who refused, on the grounds that the feeling between us was not strong enough for marriage. I offered to give her my name, even so, but she would have none of it. She has always been the most strong-minded of women in refusing to compromise her true feelings.'

'Indeed,' I murmured, 'I can well believe it.'

Lord Carstairs sighed heavily, and continued. 'I always believed that I had paid the price for my selfish behaviour, if such it was, by being denied the opportunity to see my son or to have a hand in his upbringing, beyond the regular sums of money which I naturally contributed for his education up until his twenty-first year. I then made him a handsome settlement...but I do not say this to justify myself. I have no other child, you know; that means, of course, that officially I am childless. It is a great sorrow to my wife, and you will understand, gentlemen, that I have never been able to bring myself to disclose to her the incidents of my past life, or the existence of my son. This present business would kill her, if she ever got to hear of it.'

'She will never hear of it,' said Holmes calmly, 'if only we can act quickly. Now, Lord Carstairs, suppose you tell me the details: do you know the identity of your blackmailer?'

'No. He remains quite anonymous. He signs himself only by the letters Q.B.'

'The letters Q.B. Hmm.'

Holmes closed his eyes and furrowed his brow in concentration, obviously racking his memory for some clue or connection. After a while, he was evidently forced to give up with a shrug.

'He communicates with you in writing, then? Do you have his letters?'

'I have so far received two. The first one I tried, perhaps unwisely, to ignore. I hoped, I suppose, that the threat it contained was not worth taking seriously; though I did take the unwarranted step of writing to my son to warn him. Since contacting Maurice, I received a second letter. It was this that determined me to come up to London. Maurice, it transpired, had already written to Maria about it. Upon my contacting him the second time, he sent her a telegram, so that we could all three arrange to meet.'

'I have seen the telegram. May I see the letters?'

For answer, Lord Carstairs rose and went over to a locked desk that stood in the corner of the room. He extracted a key from his pocket, opened the desk, and took out two letters, which he handed silently to Holmes.

'Ah,' said Holmes, turning one of them over and inspecting the envelope without attempting to extract the letter, 'posted in South London on the 2nd of January. Carefully addressed; printed in capitals, not handwritten — that is to be expected. The envelope has been smoothed out carefully after the letter was inserted. This correspondent is a person of calm and determination. So.'

Carefully he withdrew the letter. 'Also printed in capitals,' he murmured. 'Hmm. Q.B. knows what he is about; capitals are easy to disguise and hard to decipher. There is a certain slant to them, however; I wonder — but we must not be hasty. Dated the 1st of January; I note that he refrains from wishing you a Happy New Year. Hmm.'

He perused the letter in silence for a short while, then handed it to me.

'Watson,' he said, 'be good enough to read it aloud, if you would. That way we may better judge its tone.'

I obeyed.

> My dear Lord Carstairs,
>
> I have a proposition to put to you, which I think may be of some interest. I have in my possession two letters written by yourself to the late Mr Charles Courtney, upon the occasion of your wedding, dated the 25th of April 1876 and the 4th of August 1876 respectively. They contain references of a personal nature which I am sure you would not wish to make public.
>
> Might I trouble you for a small remuneration? £2,000 would be adequate. I am afraid it will have to be cash.
>
> I shall expect your reply within two weeks, to be forwarded to the Post Office at Dulwich Village by no later than the 14th of January.
>
> I will then contact you again with the details.
>
> Q.B.
>
> P.S. I hope that your son is well?'

Holmes listened to my reading with half-closed eyes.

'Hmm, hmm. Would you object, Lord Carstairs, to my smoking?'

'Not at all.'

In deference to his surroundings, Holmes took out his cigarette case, having taken the letter as I handed it back to him and smoothed it out carefully onto the arm of the chair. Drawing gratefully on his cigarette, he proceeded to examine the second envelope.

'You say you ignored this first letter, Lord Carstairs?' he said casually.

'I'm afraid I did. My idea was to refuse to be drawn into the matter. I suppose that I hoped the blackmailer would lose his nerve.'

'A pity. You might have been able to find out something very interesting at Dulwich Post Office; though I'm sure that such a meticulous correspondent would not collect his mail in person. Now, what have we here?'

He had extracted the second letter and smoothed it out upon his knee. After reading it, he passed it over for my perusal, indicating that I was to read it aloud. It was shorter than the first, and dated the 14th of January.

> My dear Lord Carstairs,
>
> So you choose to ignore my little proposition? I am sure the gossip columns will be grateful to you.
>
> I give you one last opportunity. Have £2,000 ready in used notes in a plain briefcase, and bring it with you to the clock at Waterloo Station at 6.00 p.m. on the 24th of January.
>
> Wait there for fifteen minutes. I would strongly advise you to come alone.
>
> Q.B.
>
> P.S. I trust that Lady Carstairs is in good health, and well able to cope with a little excitement?

Lord Carstairs gave a groan as he heard the last sentence. 'It was that that decided me,' he said. 'My wife is far from robust, and the shock of such a disclosure could kill her. There was nothing else for it, Mr Holmes. I contacted my son for the second time, and came to London. He, Maria and I are all agreed that there is nothing to be done but comply with the arrangements set out in the letter. I have the money ready. The 24th of January is the day after tomorrow, and I intend to be at Waterloo Station, alone, at 6.00 p.m. with the money ready to hand over.'

Holmes drew on his cigarette, and sat silently for some time. At length he said, 'What was in these letters, Lord Carstairs, which

Q.B. has in his possession?'

'They are addressed to my late friend, Mr Charles Courtney, of whose sad and untimely death you may have read last year. He died of consumption, last August; he was two years younger than myself. He was the best friend a man ever had, and I would have trusted him with my life.'

'Evidently you did trust him with your secret.'

'My dear sir, he knew all about it from the first! He was my support and my adviser over the whole affair. He was also the best man at my wedding, which as you may gather, took place some ten years ago, and it was on this occasion that I wrote him the fatal letters.'

'Can you remember exactly the compromising words?'

'Almost exactly. The first was written some months before my wedding, when preparations were still at an early stage. I invited him to be best man, and made some light-hearted reference to the fact that I would have to give up my old easy ways and become a model of virtue as a married man; adding, on a serious note, that I would have to give up all hope of future contact with my son, which I saw to be a painful but necessary decision.'

'I see. And the second letter?'

'The second letter was written a few days before the ceremony itself. It was mainly concerned with travel arrangements. Towards the end I made some reference to his own last letter to me, which had contained some sympathetic words of advice. I said something like: "Thank you for your kind words about my boy; as you say, he is in good hands, and my contributions will ensure a good education. For the rest, it must be as you say; mum's the word." '

Sherlock Holmes remained relaxed back in his chair, eyes half closed.

'I see,' he repeated. 'And in neither letter was your son's name or that of his mother mentioned?'

'No. I am absolutely certain as to that, thank God!'

'Very well. We may assume that Q.B. is working in the dark as to your son's identity. Now we come to the crux of the matter; how did these letters pass into his hands, and have you any clue as to who he is?'

Lord Carstairs sighed. 'I have wracked my brains over the matter and come up with nothing conclusive. When Courtney died, all his personal effects would have gone into his sister's possession, she being his only surviving relative. He was a bachelor.'

'Do you know this sister?'

'Not well, but enough to believe that she would never stoop to blackmail. And what reason would she have? She is rich enough, since her brother's death; and I am certainly not aware of any grudge she may bear against me.'

'Her name?'

'Mrs Cecil Forrester.'

'Ah, she has a husband.'

'She has been a widow these three years. Her husband died in India.'

'I see. And have there been subsequent suitors?'

Lord Carstairs seemed somewhat embarrassed by the question.

'Well...as to that,' said he, stroking his moustache with a look of indecisive amusement upon his face, 'there... appears to have been a development in the lady's life. Rather a topical one, I suppose, under the circumstances. Rumour has it that she has been heard on more than one occasion to declare herself utterly opposed to anything of the kind. She appears to prefer the company of her intimate friends. I'm sure, under the circumstances, that I need explain no further...'

He must have thought it very prim of me (under the circumstances) to blush, but blush I did.

Sherlock Holmes opened his eyes very wide, and leaned forward in his chair.

'Good heavens, Lord Carstairs, do I understand you to imply that this Mrs Forrester moves in circles in which she could well have made the acquaintance of Miss Kirkpatrick and of your — well, and of Miss D'Arcy, for example?'

'Ah, I have forestalled you there, Mr Holmes,' said Lord Carstairs with a wry chuckle. 'I have discussed the whole thing with Maria. She has heard of Mrs Forrester, she says, but she has not actually met her; even though, coincidentally, she also resides in Camberwell. No, the problem must definitely be approached from my end, Mr Holmes. However the blackmailer obtained the letters from Mrs Forrester, he is definitely not on Maria's trail. If he knew that my son was also hers, he would certainly make no secret of the fact, as it would add scandal to scandal.'

'Hmm.' Holmes lit a second cigarette. The firelight played across his tense features, giving them an unearthly, almost a threatening quality, I thought. 'Mrs Cecil Forrester is definitely the link in the chain, however,' he said. 'It may be true, as you say, that she herself would not blackmail her brother's old friend, especially as her own social position appears to be somewhat unsteady. Who would be most likely, therefore, to have had access to Mrs Forrester's papers over the last few months? Clearly someone with whom she is intimate. From what you say, Lord Carstairs, that person is unlikely to be of the male gender. The chances of the blackmailer being a woman are therefore very high.

'There is always the possibility, of course, that those letters have been stolen from her; so we must not exclude the male gender entirely from our enquiry...Surely, Lord Carstairs, your natural curiosity must have led you to try and contact Mrs Forrester? I am assuming from what you have said, that you have not been successful in this.'

Lord Carstairs gave a short laugh. 'Upon making enquiries, I found that Mrs Forrester is out of the country. I believe that she intends to spend the rest of the winter in Paris, where she has a friend; but exactly where in Paris, and with which friend, I have been unable to ascertain. Obviously the letters I have received do not come from Paris! And now there is no more time.'

Sherlock Holmes rose briskly from his chair.

'There are forty-eight hours, Lord Carstairs,' he said. 'And those forty-eight hours may be everything. Thank you for this late interview — I trust you will have no reason to regret it. I will be in touch with you again by the morning of the 24th at the very latest. In the meantime, I would advise you to do nothing yourself, and to discourage Miss and Mr Kirkpatrick from any further attempts at burglary. Good evening to you, Lord Carstairs.'

He had already shaken hands with the bemused gentleman and was halfway to the door before our host had time to express the bewilderment caused by these parting words.

'Burglaries?' he faltered. 'What burglaries, Mr Holmes?'

I hastened to reassure him as I shook his hand.

'Mr Maurice Kirkpatrick made an attempt to procure his birth certificate from his mother's house at Camberwell this morning,' I said. 'I'm afraid he was unsuccessful; the housemaid interrupted him, and the document was eventually found by Miss D'Arcy and myself. I must confess, I don't see that the possession of it would have done him much good.'

Lord Carstairs gave a rueful laugh of relief.

'Good heavens, Dr Watson! I suppose they wanted to forestall any similar attempts on the part of the blackmailer. But as I have said, I am sure there is no reason to fear an approach from that side. So, Miss D'Arcy holds the document?'

'Well — ' I hesitated. 'No, actually it is in Mr Holmes' possession.

But I assure you that it will be returned to Miss Kirkpatrick once this affair is all over. I have every confidence,' I added reassuringly, 'that Mr Sherlock Holmes will soon have the matter cleared up.'

Lord Carstairs shook my hand warmly.

'My dear Dr Watson,' he said, 'I really am most grateful both to Mr Holmes and to you. I must say that I read your account of Mr Holmes' handling of the Mormon business with the greatest interest, and like you, I have every confidence in him. I only wish I had had the good sense to consult him at the beginning of this affair.'

With that, he bade us a hearty farewell, and we left him a much more cheerful man than we had found him.

## — *VIII* —

IT WAS PAST midnight by the time we reached Baker Street. Holmes made straight for the spirit flask on the sideboard.

'You're not tired, Watson?' he said, as he poured two very large whiskies and soda.

I was, in fact, at the stage where one is too tired for sleep; my excesses of the previous evening (was it only the previous evening?), my broken night, followed by the excitement of the last fourteen hours or so, had reduced me to a state of remarkable lucidity. The adrenaline pulsed through my veins, and my whole body felt light and transparent.

'Not at all, Holmes,' I murmured; and accepting the proffered glass, I sank into the armchair with a sigh.

Holmes curled himself up in his chair and lit a pipe. For some time he stared at the contents of his glass as though he expected to read there the identity of the mysterious 'Q.B.'

'Well, Watson,' he said at last, removing his pipe from his mouth and downing half of his whisky at one gulp, 'what do you make of it?'

'It is certainly...unusual,' I said dreamily, holding up my glass to catch the light, as though it were the whisky we were discussing.

'Q.B., Q.B.,' muttered Holmes. 'Somewhere in my memory, Watson, is the key that will unlock the door to Q.B.'s identity. I know it. I sense it; and yet I cannot — quite — reach it.'

He remained curled cat-like in the chair, shrouded in smoke from his pipe.

'So,' he continued, 'we will have to take the long road. We will have to start with Mrs Cecil Forrester. By all accounts, a very interesting lady.'

'But she is in Paris!'

'Quite so. Your capacity to absorb information, my good Watson, never ceases to amaze me. I, too, had registered the fact that she is in Paris, as Lord Carstairs so kindly informed us.'

'All right, all right,' I interrupted peevishly. 'I was only thinking aloud. I suppose that, geographically speaking, we should begin our search somewhere in the region of Dulwich Village.'

'My dear fellow, you scintillate tonight!'

'We could enquire first at Mrs Forrester's Camberwell address, of course,' I continued, ignoring him, 'or we could enquire among her friends. Obviously Miss Kirkpatrick is not of her circle, but I wonder if Miss D'Arcy herself would be able to help us? She said to me that some of her best friends had been married women.'

'My dear Watson — ' began Holmes, and stopped short. Since I had determined, in my elated state, to ignore him, I took no notice.

'Of course, if we were to approach Miss D'Arcy we would have to disclose the whole situation to her; Lord Carstairs' role in the matter, I mean. And that could be painful for her. On the other hand, surely the truth cannot be kept from her now; she is bound to put the question to Miss Kirkpatrick in no uncertain terms when she returns — '

'Be quiet, man, for heaven's sake!' cried Holmes, uncurling himself with swift agility and springing up from his chair. I looked at him reproachfully, as he downed the remainder of his glass and began to pace the room.

'There is no need, Holmes — ' I began, but he cut me short with an impatient wave of his hand.

'Shush, Watson. You have given me the clue. What a blind fool I was not to think of it immediately! Pass me the reference book.'

Meekly I extracted the bulky volume from its place on Holmes' bookshelf and handed it to him. I watched him as he sat perched on the edge of his chair, balancing the book on his knees, hunched over it in a hungry attitude like a bird of prey ready to swoop and devour. He turned the pages swiftly, until he froze suddenly, drawing in his breath in a low hiss of excitement.

Well?' I asked impatiently.

He raised his eyebrows and surveyed me long and searchingly.

'Watson,' he said, 'tell me truthfully, has it ever occurred to you that I may be past my prime? Is it possible, do you think, that I am losing my grip? That I could be experiencing softening of the brain?'

'Never, Holmes!' I cried loyally, much amazed. 'Unless,' I added cunningly, after a moment's thought, 'it could be that your indulgence in the cocaine habit has had a dulling effect upon — '

'Never mind, Watson,' he interrupted with a dismissive gesture. 'Let us stick to the point. If my suspicions are correct, this is a most extraordinary — however, it is always a mistake to theorise in advance of the evidence. One thing is certain, however, Watson. We are looking for a woman who calls herself the Queen Bee.'

For a moment, I wondered whether he might not really be experiencing softening of the brain after all. I stared at him in a questioning manner. He chuckled, and tapped with his long finger at the open page on his knee.

'The Queen Bee, my dear Watson, is an adventuress of doubtful reputation whom it has not yet been my privilege to encounter, but whose details I thought it worthwhile to enter here, having heard her mentioned in several interesting contexts in the course of my career. She is known to be of good family, though they have long since ceased to recognise her, and she does not use the family name. She appears to have several questionable sources of income, and to operate with what I gather to be considerable charm and flair, in the circles to which the French give the interesting designation of the *demi-monde*. She takes the greatest pleasure in bringing the wealthy and respectable to account for their past misdeeds; no doubt her past treatment at the hands of respectable society has something to do with that. She is known to reside in South London.

'That she is the blackmailer of Lord Robert Carstairs is entirely plausible. In fact it is more than plausible; it is certain.'

I walked across to the sideboard and absent-mindedly poured myself a second whisky and soda.

'I have never heard of her,' I said thoughtfully.

'I would hardly expect you to have heard of her. You do not move in the right circles, my dear Watson.'

I gave a short, harsh laugh which caused my friend to raise his eyebrows. 'At any rate,' I said, taking a hasty gulp from my glass, 'I would be surprised if Miss D'Arcy has not heard of her.'

Holmes leaned back and surveyed me coolly.

'How your thoughts do run on that young lady,' he remarked drily. 'She seems to have quite a hold over you. I hope that you have not taken her too far into your confidence.'

'Don't be ridiculous, Holmes,' I said, blushing hotly. Something in his tone made me feel uneasy.

He continued to regard me from his chair. 'Well, well,' he said at last, 'I shall investigate the activities of the Queen Bee tomorrow. And I think, Watson, that it would be better *not* to approach Miss D'Arcy at this stage. In fact, I would strongly advise complete discretion where that lady is concerned.

'It really is most gratifying,' he continued, rising and sauntering slowly across to the sideboard, 'to have such an opportunity to investigate the activities of a person who has hitherto remained in the wings, as it were, in every drama in which I have participated so far. Most gratifying,' he repeated, crossing to the mantelpiece, glass in hand, to refill his pipe. 'And most thought-provoking.'

I could see that he was determined to ignore me until I took the hint and went to bed. He himself was preparing for an all-night sitting. What could I do then, but take the hint? With one last, meaningful glance at the morocco case which still lay upon the mantelpiece, I bade him good night and retired, giddy and exhausted from lack of sleep and emotional strain.

When I descended to breakfast the next morning, feeling considerably refreshed and in a stronger frame of mind, I found Sherlock Holmes standing by the window, hastily drinking a cup of coffee. I had to look twice to be sure that it was really he, for he was dressed as a young man of the respectable working class, in a threadbare dark suit, somewhat shiny at the elbows, with a red muffler at his throat. A cloth cap lay upon the chair.

At my entrance he turned to face me, with the slight swagger that he always adopted as part and parcel of disguises of this sort.

'Ah, Watson,' said he, 'I trust that you are feeling the better for a good night's sleep?'

I nodded my assent, and surveyed him with a questioning air.

'As you perceive, we meet in passing this morning,' he continued. 'I fear I must leave you to breakfast alone. I go to hunt the Queen Bee.'

I knew better than to question him as to his precise plans or direction. 'Well, Holmes, I wish you good hunting,' I said, as I poured myself some coffee and glanced at the breakfast table, which had barely been disturbed.

'Thank you, dear fellow.'

He was in excellent humour. He passed behind me as I reached for the toast and pinched my arm.

'You may expect me back this afternoon,' he said. 'And then, if I am not much mistaken, we will be able to discuss the best method of drawing the Queen Bee's sting.'

With that, he was gone.

I remained standing with my back to the door, and absent-mindedly ate several pieces of dry toast. After a while, I recovered myself and resorted to a more civilised breakfast, accompanied by a hasty perusal of *The Times*. When Mrs Hudson called to clear away the breakfast things, I still remained in my chair, lost in thought. By the time I eventually raised my eyes to the clock, it was half past ten.

I rose with deliberation and went to ring for my boots. It was no use, I thought, as I donned my coat and hat. My stronger frame of mind had not effected a lessening of the torment within me. But it had aided me to form a resolve to tackle the matter.

Once in the street, I hailed a hansom, and gave a direction to Camberwell Grove. I was going to call on the one person with whom I felt that I could speak freely. Whatever Holmes' reservations about her, I was going to have a further talk with Miss D'Arcy.

## — *IX* —

IT WAS THE housemaid, Hetty, who opened the door to me. She looked at me expectantly, obviously in hopes that I brought some news. I shook my head briefly, and asked whether her mistress were at home and would see me.

Miss D'Arcy lost no time in joining me in the drawing room. She looked tense and anxious, but otherwise appeared to be bearing up well. It was only as she began to question me that I realised in how awkward a position I had placed myself by this unscheduled visit. What progress had we made? Had we seen Maria's son? Who was blackmailing him? Had we seen Maria?

Since Holmes had seen fit to disclose to her his intention to visit Mr Maurice Kirkpatrick, I saw no objection to enlightening her on that score at least. I treated her to an amusing description of that gentleman and his residence, and assured her that we had indeed seen Miss Kirkpatrick, and that she appeared in good health and tolerably calm, although obviously under considerable strain. On the subject of our actual progress, however, I thought it wisest to be reticent. This was difficult, as Miss D'Arcy was most persistent, especially upon the subject of the blackmail hypothesis; and in the end I was obliged to feign ignorance myself, saying that although I knew that Mr Sherlock Holmes had the matter well in hand, and that I had every hope that he would bring it to a successful conclusion very soon, he had not taken me into his confidence as to the exact nature of his investigations — which was true inasmuch as it referred to his activities of that morning.

One point I did let slip, however; I revealed that it was not Mr Maurice Kirkpatrick, but his father who was the victim of blackmail.

Miss D'Arcy looked so extremely shocked that I wondered whether I should once again take the liberty of offering her some of her own brandy. Her eyes resumed that glassy stare that I had observed when Holmes had first mentioned the possibility of blackmail. I assumed that she did not like to hear mention of a gentleman who had been so intimately involved in her friend's past, and tried to find some words of reassurance.

'So you see, in a way it is not really Miss Kirkpatrick's concern at all,' I said. 'It is extremely doubtful that the blackmailer knows her identity; and it was only her son who saw fit to involve her in the matter, rather unwisely in my opinion.'

Miss D'Arcy silenced me with an impatient gesture. She had risen and crossed over to the window, where she stood in evident agitation.

'Who is his father?' she asked lightly, though her attitude betrayed her. I shifted uneasily in my chair. I had already said far too much, and the violence of her reaction warned me that it would be unwise to reveal more.

'Well...I'm so sorry, Miss D'Arcy, but I really don't think it is my place to tell you that. I'm sure Miss Kirkpatrick will tell you herself, when she returns; that must be enough for you. Holmes would never forgive me, if I were to commit so serious a breach of professional confidence...'

I trailed off unhappily, and lowered my gaze, twisting my hands in my lap. Miss D'Arcy went to the sideboard and poured us both a drink. Unconventional as such hospitality was in a lady, I accepted mine gratefully.

'So, Mr Sherlock Holmes is on the trail of a blackmailer,' she said, striding about the room in a most unladylike manner.

'Yes; and I can assure you, Miss D'Arcy, that he will not rest until he has found — the person he is looking for. In a couple of days at most, the whole matter will be cleared up and Miss Kirkpatrick will be home again. There really is no need to worry.'

My assurance seemed to do nothing to soothe her. I began to feel no small annoyance towards Holmes for having forbidden me to take Miss D'Arcy into our confidence; after all, what harm could it do? She was bound to hear the whole story sooner or later, and at this stage she could even be of help to us, if she knew anything of Mrs Cecil Forrester.

Thus I began to speculate uneasily as to what Holmes would say if he knew where I was. I had to admit to myself that I had made a rather foolish and impulsive move in visiting Miss D'Arcy at all. Why had I come? I appeared only to have added to her distress, and certainly she would now be in no mood to help me in mine.

It was as though she could read my mind, for she suddenly stopped her pacing, reseated herself and fixed me again with that hard questioning stare.

'Dr Watson,' said she, 'why have you come to visit me, if you have no definite news for me, and no intention of giving me any useful information?'

I sighed and fidgeted uncomfortably in my chair.

'I am sorry, Miss D'Arcy, it was certainly most ill-advised of me,' I said at last. 'The fact is that I had some idea of asking your advice on — on a personal matter. Since you had already been so sympathetic, I thought — but I see now that it was very selfish of me, and you are certainly in no fit state to be bothered with my affairs. I think perhaps it would be best if I leave right away.'

I did not raise my eyes to her face until I had finished speaking, and then I saw that her expression had changed completely; she was relaxed, and smiling — one could almost say, relieved.

'Oh, my dear Dr Watson, it is I who must apologise,' said she. 'I had assumed that you had come on official rather than personal business. I wish you had put me right immediately. Of course, I will be more than happy to listen to you, and to give you any advice that it is in my power to give. You have already been so kind, and I would be ungrateful indeed if I were to refuse to help you in return.'

I warmed to these kind words, and thanked her. She offered me another brandy, and under its influence I felt my inhibitions melt away, and I began to speak once more of my feelings for Mr Sherlock Holmes. Miss D'Arcy listened in silence, questioning me only when necessary in the interests of clarity.

The picture that I painted was bleak indeed; it was one of hopeless infatuation, coupled of course with guilt and fear which are the inevitable counterpart to such inclinations in our present unenlightened age. Miss D'Arcy, of course, was well aware from her own experience of much of what I was suffering. When I had finished speaking, she asked me one or two questions concerning Sherlock Holmes himself; his moods, his conversation, his treatment of me in private and in public. She even probed me about his use of certain substances, and my concern over his habit made me perhaps more forthcoming upon the subject than I should have been.

Miss D'Arcy sat in silence for some time when she had finished questioning me, as though trying to come to some decision. Then she looked up at me with a determined expression.

'Dr Watson,' said she, 'I like you, and respect your integrity, and you have paid me a great compliment in taking me voluntarily into your confidence in this way. Whatever the future may reveal, I want you to remember that. Now, I have one assurance, and one piece of advice to give you.

'The assurance is that Mr Sherlock Holmes feels much for you, and is more dependent on you, in a sense, than you are upon him. Why else would he provoke you, as he does, why else would he administer drugs to himself in your presence, if he does not want to stimulate your reaction, and be assured of your concern? He gives to you, and to you alone, all his vulnerable side, all his needs, all his love, so far as he is able; and yet, unless I am much mistaken, he will never give you more than he gives at present. He is incapable of it; there exists in him some deep emotional blockage, some fatal inability to admit to his vulnerable side, which causes him to present himself as all brain and no heart. However, the cost of this is high, as his need for the drug bears witness.

'Now, I do not believe that you will change him; and as far as I can see, if you let matters remain as they are, he will hurt you badly. Of his basic preference for his own sex, and his indifference to mine, I have no doubt whatever. But rather than accept himself, he will be cruel, even to the one he loves. You, Dr Watson, are more stable than he, and unless I am much mistaken, more naturally versatile. You are also, by virtue of your being more demonstrative and self-accepting, more at risk.

'I do not know if you are aware, Dr Watson, that a certain Bill, namely the Criminal Law Amendment Bill, was passed in January of last year, and is now law? It contains a section — Section 11, entitled "Outrages on Public Decency" — which puts you, and all the companions with whom I have observed you, in considerable danger.'

I felt the blood drain from my face.

'I have heard of it,' I said. 'I have — not enquired as to the details...'

Miss D'Arcy waited until I raised my eyes to hers, and then held my gaze as she continued. 'It refers exclusively to your own sex, with no mention of mine — a fact which has several implications which I will not go into here. Briefly, Section 11 states that all acts of a certain nature between men — *all* acts, Dr Watson, as was not the case before — whether committed in public or in private, are liable to a punishment of up to two years' imprisonment with hard labour.

'I see, Dr Watson,' she continued, watching my face, 'that you understand the implications. I am so sorry. You may be surprised at my knowing these details; don't be. I make it my business to know the exact loophole and letter of the law as regards every aspect of personal conduct.

'I am telling you this simply to make sure that you are aware of the risks you run. I am sure I do not need to add, that even if his own nature did not prevent him from doing so, his knowledge of this law — and I think we may assume that he does know of it — would prevent Mr Sherlock Holmes from changing his behaviour towards you, no matter what his feelings.

'When you confided in me yesterday, I spoke lightly of the advisability of protecting one's reputation. I did not then feel inclined, on so slight an acquaintance, to take the trouble to speak more urgently to you on the matter. Since then it has preyed on my mind, and your honouring me with your further confidence decides me.

'Put yourself above suspicion, Dr Watson. Take a wife, set up your own establishment. You can do it, as many have done before you. It will be hard, both for you and for him; but if you do not make this sacrifice now, you will be both at risk. It is my belief that Sherlock Holmes will in any case sacrifice you to his own instability one day; and you will only be able to bear it if you have a life of your own to fall back on. I do not say that you should end your association with him; only that you should take steps to put it on a different footing. You are vulnerable, Dr Watson, in many ways; I urge you to take this step now, before it is too late!'

The reader will readily imagine with what emotion I heard her words. I remember staring hard at a small occasional table that stood slightly to the right of my chair, on which lay three neatly addressed letters ready for the post, and knowing that the sight would be branded forever onto my memory of this conversation. Curiously, I remained dry-eyed, but I must have paled considerably, for Miss D'Arcy handed me a third glass of brandy and softly urged me to drink it. I sipped at it absently, and sighed.

'Miss D'Arcy,' I said at last, 'I thank you for being so frank with me. I think you may be right. I am sure you are right. But I must take a little time; it seems so vast a step — so irrevocable...'

'Not irrevocable,' she interrupted quietly. 'Not at all irrevocable. But prudent.'

I sighed again.

'Well,' I said, 'I will think it over. At least, I will think over setting up on my own, I suppose. But as for marriage — how can I possibly contemplate such a step? I could never dismiss him from my mind enough to act the part of the married man. And who on earth would want to marry me?'

'Oh, as to that, Dr Watson, an attractive man like yourself will have no trouble. Only take care, and choose a sympathetic wife. Let your natural discrimination be your guide. And one further piece of advice — when you are married, take care that you advertise the fact. Write your romance into one of Mr Holmes' cases, if necessary; make sure that it is entirely plausible to your public. That way you will safeguard both your reputation and his.'

Once again, I absorbed the advice, and thanked her.

'You have been very good to me, Miss D'Arcy. I do not know quite how to express my gratitude to you.'

'All I ask in the way of thanks, Dr Watson, is that you do not withdraw your trust from me; that you continue to believe that for you, I have only the greatest affection and respect, and that I will never betray your confidence.'

'Miss D'Arcy, how could I ever think anything else?'

She turned away with a slight shrug, and the next moment the door to the room was opened, and John, the footman, came in bearing a telegram.

'For you, sir,' he said.

I rose unsteadily, and opened it with a sense of foreboding not unmixed with guilt.

'RETURN AT ONCE. S.H.,' I read.

'Ah,' I said, showing the message to Miss D'Arcy, 'I expect this means progress. Undoubtedly he must be hot on the trail.'

Miss D'Arcy gave a wry smile as she read the summons. 'Did you tell Mr Holmes that you were coming here?' she asked.

'No,' I answered nervously, 'I did not. But he always finds me.'

I laughed unconvincingly. The telegram had communicated his annoyance to both of us. I asked John to call me a cab, and prepared to take my leave. Miss D'Arcy seemed subdued, and I tried to convey to her a sense of optimism, in return for her kindness.

'I am sure,' I said, 'that we will soon have some good news for you. In the meantime, I will take my leave — and thank you for your concern and for your advice, Miss D'Arcy. I really am most grateful.'

'Goodbye, Dr Watson,' was all she said.

I travelled back to Baker Street in a state of most painful agitation. Undoubtedly, I could expect a cold welcome from Holmes. How had he known where to contact me? And how was I going to face him with equanimity, with Miss D'Arcy's words still fresh in my mind? The brandy was making me feel light-headed, and I realised that I was hungry and that it was past lunch-time, and that lunch would almost certainly be the last thing that Holmes would suggest.

I tried to think over Miss D'Arcy's advice, but all that came into my mind was a vision of the occasional table with the three envelopes upon it. I could see them quite clearly, even down to the slant of the bold capitals in which they were addressed. Suddenly I became preoccupied with the realisation that I had seen that writing somewhere before; I recognised it as I had recognised Maurice Kirkpatrick's writing the previous day. But this was, presumably, Miss D'Arcy's hand; I must have seen it by chance, earlier, it was as simple as that.

It is a strange fact that small worries can push great ones aside in the midst of the worst crises; try as I would, I could not get the writing out of my mind. Finally, annoyed at myself for being bothered so unaccountably by something so trivial, I adopted the simple visual method of imagining myself looking at the envelope, and then raising my eyes from it to see in what surroundings I found myself.

I found myself, as the reader will have surmised, in Lord Carstairs' sitting room.

By the time the cab arrived at Baker Street, I had had ample opportunity fully to appreciate my situation. It was some moments before I could bring myself to alight, and several more before I could summon the physical and moral strength to climb the stairs to our rooms.

# — X —

I PAUSED AGAIN at the door, to prepare myself; but even that brief respite was denied me, for it was flung open and there, wreathed in smoke, his pipe in his mouth and an expression on his face that I can only describe as that of a particularly wrathful and sadistic headmaster, stood Sherlock Holmes.

With a jerk of his head he motioned me inside. Unsteadily I crossed the room and collapsed into a chair by the fireplace. Holmes, having closed the door, came and stood directly in front of me. I noted that he had changed back into his own clothes already, and from the thickness of the smoke in the room, I gathered that he had been back for some time.

I gazed up at him with what I hoped was a look of hopeless appeal.

'You can cut that out, Watson,' he said icily, 'and concentrate your energies upon giving me an explanation, if you possess one, of exactly what you think you were doing at Camberwell Grove.'

'How did you deduce that I was there?' I stalled.

Holmes gave me a look of most cutting disdain. 'My dear Watson, I did not have to deduce it. I saw you arrive there with my own eyes.'

My jaw dropped. 'But — when?...How?' I stammered.

He blew a vicious cloud of smoke at me.

'I saw you alight from your hansom and walk up to the front door. I was at the tradesman's entrance at the time, and unable to intercept you. Furthermore, my morning's work would have been ruined had I betrayed so much as a hint of recognition. You, needless to say, did not observe me.'

'No...well...good heavens, Holmes, how was I to know that you had gone to Miss D'Arcy's? What were you doing there?'

'I seem to remember asking you the same question, and you have not yet done me the honour to reply. However, I have no objection to explaining my activities. If you possessed an ounce of deductive ability you would be able to work it out for yourself, especially bearing in mind that I gave you a specific caution about Miss D'Arcy only last night.

'I am a young man of the name of Douglas, looking for respectable employment. I have heard that a vacancy will soon exist in Miss D'Arcy's household, due to the impending departure of her footman, Mr John Chapman, to the vicinity of his ailing mother, as you may recall.

'I decide to call on him, to sound him out about the household, and to ask whether he can put in a good word for me. I find him most friendly and amenable; we spend a good half-hour or so chatting at the tradesman's entrance. It is a quiet day, he says, and the housemaid will see to any callers.

'It's a rather queer household in some ways, he says, but the two ladies are generous employers and the duties are reasonable. I ask him what the duties consist of. He trots out the usual list, during which time I have ample opportunity to notice your arrival — not to worry, he says, the housemaid will see to you. Are there any extra or unusual duties, I ask? Well, the ladies sometimes keep unsocial hours, he says, and he and the other man have often to sit up late. Anything else? Only the mail; Miss D'Arcy sometimes has letters left for her at Dulwich Post Office and he has to collect them. Yes, it is a bit of a way out, and goodness knows she can be very secretive when she has a mind to be. He doesn't believe even Miss Kirkpatrick knows of it. Still, it's not his place, etc., and he'd advise me to take the same attitude.

'Now it's about time he got back to his duties. He'll put in a good word for me if I like, but it's not really the right time at the moment, one of the ladies has been called away from home unexpectedly, some family trouble he thinks, and it would be best to wait until things are back to normal. In any case, the ladies will probably require a written reference. That's all right, I say, I will present myself in writing, references enclosed. Will it be all right for me to mention that I have talked to him, etc.? Oh yes, of course.

'And so I come back to Baker Street, since I do not want to take the risk of hanging about the house until *you* emerge, and I despatch a telegram. Now, I trust I have made the situation sufficiently clear? Perhaps you would now care to favour me with an account of *your* morning.'

This whole narrative was delivered in clipped, sarcastic tones, and with the last sentence he almost spat at me. Crushed as I was, however, a small glow-worm of inspiration had begun to creep into the back of my mind. Was the situation clear? Yes, it had been clear to me before I entered the room. Holmes' narrative had not quite carried the shock value he had anticipated for me. How had I spent my morning? Why, when all was said and done, it had surely been no less successful than his.

I rose from my chair, and Holmes stood back to let me pass. I strolled casually across to the window.

'My morning? Why, I believe that my morning was almost as interesting as yours, my dear Holmes. As you so rightly observed, I also visited Camberwell Grove, but unlike yourself, I was not incognito. However, I did have the opportunity to make one or two observations, and I must say that I think you underestimate my deductive ability. Miss D'Arcy had inadvertently left some correspondence upon a side-table, and I was able to observe that her printing matches exactly that in the threatening letters to Lord Carstairs. I had only just time to make the observation when your telegram arrived. Extraordinary, is it not, that we should both have come to the same conclusion, and neither confided in the other?'

There was a long and ominous silence behind me. I continued to stare fixedly out of the window, not daring to turn round. A delivery of wine was being unloaded at Dolomore's across the road, and I made a desperate mental note to order myself a bottle of Château Montrose '65, if I emerged unscathed from this predicament.

Then I heard Holmes walk up softly behind me and stand so close to me that I tingled in every nerve.

'My — dear — Watson,' he hissed into my right ear, 'are you trying to tell me that you went to visit Miss D'Arcy with the sole intention of identifying her as the blackmailer of Lord Carstairs? Because if you are, let me tell you here and now that I do not believe you. Your manner when you entered the room just now was somewhat at odds with the role of successful investigator; in fact, it was more suggestive of the guilty schoolboy who has just been caught in the act.'

'Caught in the act of what?' I asked in a strained voice, as my little glow-worm of inspiration dimmed and flickered out altogether, and my bottle of claret drained upon the sands of my imagination.

I felt Holmes' cold fingers close about my wrist.

'Dear me, Watson,' he said, 'how your pulse is racing. As a medical man, you must know that deception puts a considerable strain upon the nervous system. I should definitely not advise it. Now, suppose you tell me the truth.'

There was nothing else for it but to tell the whole story, or something like it.

'I wanted to talk to her, Holmes, on a personal matter. I have a perfect right to consult her, as a friend, if I want to, and you have no right to interfere.'

'I see,' he said. He let go of my arm and I walked unsteadily back to my chair. He waited for me to seat myself, and then came and stood glaring down at me, arms akimbo.

'Very well,' he said softly. 'I have no right, as you say, to pry into your personal *affairs*' — he gave a most unpleasant emphasis to the word — 'but I have every right to prevent you from interfering in my cases. I will not ask just what you were discussing with this notorious blackmailer, except that it had better have nothing to do with me.'

His eyes searched my face menacingly. Completely crushed, I could do nothing but stare back hopelessly until his features blurred before my eyes, and I tried to blink back the tears. I heard him sigh deeply. When I looked up again, he was seated opposite me, his elbows on his knees and his chin in his hands, watching me anxiously.

'Watson,' he said gently, when my eyes met his, 'what have you done?'

'Nothing that will cause any harm to you,' I muttered.

'Why did you visit Miss D'Arcy?'

'To talk to her. We have things in common. Not blackmail.'

Holmes closed his eyes briefly and sighed again. 'Watson, Watson — do you think me completely unobservant? But did you have to give yourself away completely, and to her?'

'I haven't given anything away,' I lied desperately. 'I spoke to her as a friend. I trust her,' I added more convincingly, as I remembered her parting words. 'She promised to respect my confidence.'

'You trust a woman who is known to be a ruthless blackmailer?'

'She won't blackmail me.'

'You sound very sure of that.'

'Well,' I said, 'I am. You said yourself that the Queen Bee only stings the wealthy and the hypocritical. And besides, she has no papers of mine, or anything. And she said she has the greatest respect and affection for me.'

'And you have, in any case, done nothing for which you could be blackmailed.'

It sounded like a statement, but he raised his eyebrows questioningly. I blushed hotly and refrained from answering.

'I knew it,' he said calmly. 'My poor Watson. Why, do you imagine, do I keep myself free from entanglements of every sort? Not only because affairs of the heart are a hindrance to the logical processes of the mind, but also because I cannot afford to lay myself open in any way to the possibility that my reputation could be tarnished. I have to be above blackmail on the moral front, however unconventional I may be in the rest of my behaviour. And when it comes to morals of this particular stamp — good heavens, Watson, have you not heard of the Criminal Law Amnendment Act?'

'Yes,' I said wearily, 'Miss D'Arcy told me of it this morning.'

Even in my sorry state, I could see that once again I had surprised him.

'Miss D'Arcy? So you discussed the subject in such detail? Oh, Watson...'

For a few moments as he sat in silence nervously fingering the dead pipe in his hands, his grey eyes fixed unseeing at a point a few inches above my left shoulder, I caught an expression on his face that I had never thought to see; an expression of indecision, of wistfulness, but above all, of hopelessness. My heart lurched at the softening of his features, but sank almost immediately at the finality of the expression that settled there. As soon as his vacant eyes focussed and met mine, he dropped his gaze. He made as if to speak, and then hesitated for several long moments. At length he said, very quietly:

'My dear fellow, there is nothing I can say or do that will not — there is nothing,' he repeated, 'to be done. This hideous new law is the blackmailer's charter — it has already been called so, I believe. It will cause untold suffering, both mental and physical, and will bring about the downfall of some of the most gifted and sensitive figures of our generation. I do not intend that either you or I should be among them.

'My poor Watson,' he repeated, seeing my face, 'I see that you understand what I am trying to say. I had hoped that it went without saying. In any case, let us hope that your trust in Miss D'Arcy is justified.'

'I am sure that it is,' I said forlornly. 'She went to so much trouble to — ' I could not bring myself to say what she had advised me to do, so I said, ' — to impress on me the need for discretion. After all, she is on — our side.'

Holmes gave me a sharp look. 'Miss D'Arcy is protected by her sex,' he said, with a trace of bitterness in his voice. 'She is immune from the penalties of the law. She can use blackmail to protect herself from blackmail, if necessary. I suppose,' he continued, his voice softening somewhat, 'that she is in the unique position to wreak revenge upon such pillars of society as are responsible for Section 11.'

He thought about this for a while, and gave a rueful chuckle.

'However,' he continued seriously, 'blackmail will always remain for me a most despicable and cowardly practice, no matter what the motives; and in this present instance, Miss D'Arcy has been hoist with her own petard, wouldn't you say? I think it is high time to bring this sordid affair to a close. A short interview with the lady in question should suffice, I think, followed by a brief visit to Lord Carstairs to return his letters. The rest of the explanations will be no concern of ours, thank heaven.

'Now, Watson, this time I go to Camberwell quite alone. I absolutely forbid you to stir from the house until I come back to collect you for dinner this evening. We might dine out, I thought? No better way to celebrate the successful conclusion of a case. I shall be back by six-thirty at the latest.'

I followed him with my eyes as he disappeared into his room and emerged a minute later impeccably dressed in frock coat and top hat. I could hardly believe he was no longer angry with me. I realised that he was trying to soften the blow of his knowledge of all that went without saying; a knowledge that left me somewhat numb and dazed. I found myself repeating Miss D'Arcy's words in my mind: '...He will never give you more than he gives you at present.' And it was true, and he had almost explained it. Except that he had never admitted to feeling anything for me in the first place. His self-control, as always, was absolute.

'Don't be too harsh with her, Holmes,' I said. I felt that he judged Miss D'Arcy less kindly than she deserved. 'She obviously had no idea whom she was blackmailing. She must be feeling bad enough.'

Holmes raised his eyebrows. 'Harsh, with my client? Of course not. This whole investigation was carried out on her behalf. The fact that she also happens to be the villain of the piece is hardly my fault. However, I will not indulge in any gratuitous admonitions, if that is what you are afraid of. I will simply pocket my fee, assure her of my discretion — perhaps it will not be inappropriate to give her your regards on that point — and retire gracefully.'

'You don't have to fake my regards, Holmes,' I said, as he crossed to the door. 'I really do send them.'

He nodded briefly, and was gone.

An hour or so later, Mrs Hudson came up to light the gas, and was surprised to find me sitting alone in semi-darkness, wrapped in my thoughts.

# — XI —

TRUE TO HIS word, Holmes was back by six-thirty, and in excellent spirits, elated with his success and demurely satisfied with his financial rewards.

'Miss D'Arcy always prefers to deal in cash, she tells me,' said he, opening his wallet and showing me the wad of notes within. 'So I think, my dear Watson, that we shall dine well tonight. How about Kettner's? Would you care for an aperitif before we leave? Let me help you to a whisky and soda. My poor Watson, you look done up, anyone would think it was you who had been chasing all over London. Come now, my dear fellow, cheer up and put this whole business out of your mind. Drink up, and then go and dress. We have an evening of pure relaxation ahead of us.'

'What did she say?' I asked nervously, looking doubtfully at my glass; I was unsure as to the beneficial value of alcohol in my present state.

'Very little, in fact. She appeared to be expecting me. She even had the letters ready. I outlined the facts to her, she made no attempt to deny them, and asked me to return the letters at once to Lord Carstairs with the assurance that the proposed meeting at Waterloo Station tomorrow evening should be considered as cancelled, and that there would be no further communication. She took the opportunity to remind me that she was after all my client in this case, and would I respect her anonymity as regards all other persons involved, including Lord Carstairs? I of course assured her that once I had received my fee I would consider my involvement in the matter completely closed. I returned Mr Kirkpatrick's birth certificate to her care, and even left her his address, so that she could return it to him in person if she so desired; at any rate, she will want to contact her friend. I should imagine that those two ladies have each something to ask and something to tell one another. I also left her your regards, as I promised, which she accepted gravely, and asked me to deliver hers in return, by the way.

'I thought it best to leave immediately, and made my way to Lord Carstairs, who was, needless to say, delighted to see both me and his letters. He was curious, naturally, to know how and from whom I obtained them, but he accepted that it was a matter of professional confidence. I suspect, however, that he may make a call on Mrs Cecil Forrester when she returns from Paris. That should be interesting. Still, my dear Watson, any further developments are no concern of ours. Lord Carstairs, by the way, is a generous man, and insisted on my accepting a small financial token of his gratitude. Yes, we shall certainly dine at Kettner's, I think.'

He chuckled, and sauntered to the window. 'Now go and dress, there's a good fellow, and I shall do the same. I don't know about you, but I have eaten nothing all day, and it's remarkable what effect success and money can have upon the appetite!'

It is with regret that I must admit that the excellence of our meal that evening, and the elegance of our surroundings, failed to make any uplifting impression on me. It was the more distressing because Holmes obviously intended the whole extravagance as a treat for me, to lift my spirits and make amends for the afternoon. It was not often, in those days, that we could afford to eat at one of the more select establishments; and Holmes, in spite of his professed contempt for the social niceties, certainly possessed a penchant for the more civilised accessories of high society. He was in his element, impeccably dressed and debonair, all dazzling smiles and witty repartees. I did my best for him, but my heart was heavy with anticipation of what I had resolved to say to him that evening. The sparkling lights, the well-modulated tones of our fellow patrons' conversation, the tinkling of champagne glasses and of feminine laughter, all seemed to me to have an undertone of derision, to wear an insidious sneer. They mocked and condemned me.

Holmes' grey eyes that evening looked particularly soft and wistful to me, in contrast to his outer mood. His long white hands gestured delicately, precisely, in the air as we spoke. I sipped at my wine, and later at my coffee and curaçao, in a trance of melancholy; the dream-like quality of my surroundings mocking the end of my dreams. At length Holmes lapsed into silence also, lighting a cigarette from his silver case and leaning back pensively in his chair, letting the blue smoke drift between us. He said nothing, made no allusion to our conversation of a few hours ago. It was evident that he wanted the whole matter to sink quietly into the depths of the unspoken, so that it would never be mentioned again. '*Watson, Watson, do you think me entirely unobservant?*' He had known, then, all the time; at least, he had known something; how much, he was unlikely ever to reveal. '*My poor Watson, I see that you understand what I am trying to say; I had hoped it went without saying.*' What went without saying? That he cared for me? Or just that he had to safeguard his reputation?

Either way, it was up to me now to safeguard both our

reputations, and I had something to say that could not go without saying.

It was not until we were back at Baker Street, seated by the fire with our pipes, replete and drowsy, that I found my courage; and after all, Baker Street was the only appropriate context.

'Holmes,' I said determinedly, 'I have been thinking.'

'So I observe, my dear fellow. You have been lost in thought all evening, when you should have been enjoying yourself. You have not, if I may say so, been your usual scintillating self. In fact, were it not that the excellence of the establishment does much to supply any excitement that is lacking in one's companion, I would say that our dinner had been a failure.'

'Don't, Holmes,' I said quickly. 'I have been thinking that I should try to set up on my own. It would enable me to concentrate more upon my practice; it would be better for my career. And better for you, too. I know that I am often as much of a hindrance as a help to you. And then, bearing in mind what — what you said to me this afternoon, I think it would be better if both our reputations were not automatically linked.'

He said nothing, but took his pipe from his mouth and stared into the fire. I was amazed to see that a flush had spread over his thin cheeks. When, after nearly a minute, he still had not so much as turned to look at me, I continued speaking.

'I would still be your friend and chronicler,' I said. 'That is, if you will let me. I would still like to share in your cases, whenever you invite me to. I would still like to be your close associate. Only...'

Here I trailed off completely, and started again.

'I was not thinking of leaving immediately,' I said. 'I was thinking in terms of some time over the next few months. If I keep my eyes open, something might come up, some opportunity...and you see, you have become quite successful and well known, you no longer need to share lodgings for financial reasons...'

At last he turned to look at me. The flush had faded from his cheeks, and now he was so pale that his very lips looked white.

'My — dear Watson,' he began. For a moment he appeared to falter; then he recovered himself, and staring once more at the fire, he spoke with an hysterical rapidity.

'Of course, you must do what you think best,' he said. 'The reasons you have given for your decision are all excellent ones, and I can see no flaw in them. And you must, as you say, build up your practice; I have been very selfish in keeping you from it. I shall miss my Boswell, but — by all means, yes, you must start looking round tomorrow. I expect there are some excellent places at very reasonable rates. Dear me, I don't know what's come over me, but I am so tired. I think I shall turn in straight away. this has been an awful case. An exhausting case, that is. Good night, my dear Watson. We can discuss your plans further in the morning.'

He rose abruptly as he spoke, and turned towards his room. Not once did he look me in the eye.

I felt I could not let him go like this. I also rose, in some consternation.

'Holmes — ' I said. He turned back to me with an expression on his face such as I had never seen there before. The clear, hard eyes were dimmed, and the firm lips were shaking. He stepped towards me and for one, brief moment laid his fingers on my lips to silence me. Then he turned deliberately and took down his cocaine bottle and the morocco case from the mantelpiece. I watched him disappear into his room with them, without a word of protest.

And this is where I must end my account of the case of the Queen Bee. It has no immediate sequel, for far from discussing my proposals next day as he had promised, Holmes did not even mention the subject, either then or subsequently. Instead, he sat in his armchair with his hair-trigger and a hundred Boxer cartridges, and proceeded to adorn the opposite wall with a patriotic V.R., done in bullet holes. I watched him helplessly, knowing that there was nothing I could say that would not be better left unsaid.

It was not until several months later that an opportunity arose for me to put into practice not only the part that I had intended, but the whole of Miss D'Arcy's advice. But this sequel belongs to another story, and the curious reader may find the facts detailed in 'The Sign of Four', where I took pains to set them down, duly edited and acceptably presented for public consumption, and to publish them, first in *Lippincott's Monthly Magazine* and later in book form, with the help of my literary agent, Dr Conan Doyle. It was this gentleman who first introduced me to *The Strand* magazine, in which publication I was to have considerable success with what Holmes persisted in calling my 'highly romanticised accounts' of our joint adventures.

This account, however, has in no way been romanticised. It is the most painfully honest account that I have ever written; and it is my sincere hope that you, gentle reader of a century hence, will judge it kindly, and it will be seen to cast light rather than shadow upon the celebrated friendship between myself and Mr Sherlock Holmes.

It is always difficult — indeed, almost impossible — to set down an accurate record of the more painful events of one's life. The temptation is either to overdramatise in retrospect, or to record merely the bare bones of experience, avoiding the emotions involved.

When I wrote and published 'The Adventure of the Final Problem', and later 'The Adventure of the Empty House', I deliberately adopted the latter policy. But then I had no intention of presenting an accurate record; merely one that would satisfy the public. Even as it was, there were glaring loopholes which I had great difficulty in explaining.

Now that I come to tie up the loose ends, as it were, I will have to guide against overdoing the pathos. I hope that my future readers will forgive me; it has been a long time, in an inhospitable social climate.

John H. Watson, M.D
London, 1907

# *The Final Problem*

## — *I* —

WE SAT AT the breakfast table, my wife and I, on the morning of the 23rd of April, 1891, discussing the morning's post. Mary had received a letter from her former employer, Mrs Cecil Forrester, which had engrossed her for a full quarter of an hour; much to my relief, for I had some private correspondence of my own to peruse.

'Well, James,' she said, when she had set down her letter with a smile, 'can I help you to more coffee?'

I looked at her in some alarm. 'James?' I said.

She gestured with the coffee pot towards my letter. 'You have been using your pseudonym again,' she said. 'Dr James Watson. I am apt at reading upside down; it is a useful trick, I would advise you to cultivate it.'

'Oh, that.' I gave a nervous laugh.

'Yes, that. I wish you would tell me when you do it. It could be very awkward. Supposing the gentleman came to call on you, and I in my innocence were to disillusion him?'

I felt myself blushing, and sighed to cover my embarrassment. 'I do not think that is very likely.'

'Ah, but you should guard against all eventualities. I wonder what the maid thought when she read the envelope?'

I smiled, and sipped at my coffee. 'He asked my name. I hardly knew him. I did not give any surname at all, I don't know how he found it out.'

'He probably read "Dr J. Watson" on your hatband, or something. Did you give him our address?'

'Of course not!'

'Then how . . ?' she gestured towards the letter.

'He must have found it out . . .' I trailed off nervously, wondering how.

Mary leaned back in the chair and surveyed me anxiously.

'He is not asking you for money?'

'No, he is trying to arrange another meeting.'

'A gentleman?' She raised her eyebrows.

'Well, a soldier.'

'Ah, I see. Do be careful, John.'

'Don't worry, I will decline the invitation. There's no danger there.'

Mary picked up her own letter, and we smiled at one another. We had an easy, affectionate relationship, free from the expectations, and hence from the pitfalls, usually incumbent upon husband and wife. We liked one another, had much in common, and could guarantee one another complete freedom and discreet cover for the pursuance of our own tastes in companionship.

My published account of our wooing, in 'The Sign of Four', was accurate in one respect; it was, as has I think been remarked, a rather rapid business. But why make it otherwise? We each had nothing to lose, and much to gain from a public alliance. Mary had the blessing of her employer Mrs Forrester, whose young son was in any case fast approaching school age and no longer in need of a governess. I had wanted a similar blessing from Mr Sherlock Holmes, of course; but this I absolutely failed to procure.

'I have an invitation also,' said Mary, carefully folding her correspondence and replacing it in the envelope. 'And if it's all the same to you, I would like to accept. Isobel has invited me to spend a week at Hastings, now that the school term has started, and Valentine is out of the way.'

'That is an unkind way to speak of such a sweet little boy.'

Mary narrowed her eyes at me, and poured herself a third cup of coffee. 'I should like to leave tomorrow,' was all she said.

Isobel, of course, was none other than Mrs Cecil Forrester who had some eighteen months ago made her deceased brother's house in Hastings her permanent residence. Mary was in the habit of visiting her there regularly, and naturally I never made any demur. I lit a cigarette and smiled graciously.

'You have my permission, Mrs Watson.'

Her reply was fortunately delayed by the appearance of the maid to clear away the breakfast things. In the interval it was, I believe, somewhat modified.

'I expect you will have a visit,' she said.

I tried to look nonplussed. 'I hope not, if I refuse this invitation.'

'You know perfectly well who I mean,' she said severely, pursing her lips. 'And I will tell you in advance that I thank him for his kind enquiries and send my regards.'

'How civilised, to be sure. But I do not expect to see him, Mary. I believe he is still in France.'

'If he knows I am away, he will turn up as sure as day follows night. John, do try to make him understand that I would never stand on my position — that I would always be pleased to see him. Good heavens, I owe him enough. And he knows — he *knows* he has no reason to resent me.'

I sighed. 'Ah, my dear,' I said, 'there is nothing I can say to make him change his attitude, because he would never admit to resentment in the first place. Sometimes I suspect that the circumstances make no difference to him. I have left him, and he sees no further than that. Even though he admitted with his own lips that he could give me no reason to stay. I had hoped it would be different, but there is nothing to be done.'

Mary sighed also and rose from the table. As she passed me she reached for my hand and clasped it sympathetically.

'I am so sorry, John,' she said. 'It seems that you have not done so well out of this arrangement as I have.'

'Oh, I do pretty well, on the whole,' I said nonchalantly, giving a reassuring squeeze to her hand. 'After all, I am a rising star in the medical profession, with my own establishment, an unusually harmonious marriage, and some extremely interesting and talented friends. I sometimes rub shoulders with the rich and famous, did you know?'

'Yes, so you keep telling me. But you have not yet produced one invitation to a first night.'

'Be patient, Mrs Watson, be patient.'

She laughed and left the room. I knew that she was going to pack.

My smile faded when she had gone, and I lit a second cigarette. Against hope, I wondered whether I might indeed expect a visit from Sherlock Holmes. I had received two notes from him over the last three months, dated from Narbonne and from Nîmes, from which I gathered that his stay in France was likely to be a long one; though he did not tell me more than what I had read for myself in the newspapers, namely that he had been engaged by the French government upon a matter of supreme importance.

Still, he had not forgotten me. He had written, twice. He wanted me to know where he was, what he was doing.

In the early days of my marriage, several times I had tried to invite him to dinner. Only once had I succeeded, and the occasion had not been a success. He was very cordial to Mary, a civilised guest in every way; but when left alone with me at the dinner table, he fell into a sulk and refused to relax. I see now that it was insensitive of me to attempt to patronise him with these invitations, and I can understand his rejection of them. Knowing as I did the insecurity that lay behind the precise, logical facade, it was unfair of me to flaunt my new security. Knowing as he did the real reasons for my flight into marriage, it was unfair of him to be so resentful.

And yet the passage of three years had not made any difference to his attitude. He would visit me, as Mary said, uninvited and at odd hours, either when she was from home, or when the hour was so late that he knew she had in all probability retired to bed. He would smoke my tobacco, make comments upon my appearance and amuse himself by deducing how I had spent my day, whether I had had any other visitors lately, the state of my health, etc. He would then ask casually whether 'Mrs Watson' were in, and upon receiving the expected reply, would invariably request that I abandon my practice for the next few days and accompany him upon whichever investigation was currently in hand.

I had, as I have mentioned elsewhere, an 'accommodating neighbour' in Dr Anstruther, who could usually be prevailed upon to cover for me on these occasions; but I think that I would have followed Holmes at a moment's notice, even if it had meant losing my practice altogether. Time and marriage had not altered my feelings for him; and I, grasping at straws, was pleased to read in his minute observations of me, his constant reminders that he 'knew my habits', the confidence and alacrity with which he summoned me from my home and work, and even in his unreasonable jealousy of poor Mary, a sign of that affection for me which he had never allowed himself to express.

Sometimes, if he knew that Mary were at home, he would summon me by telegram to his side. I always went, however inconvenient the time. Mary understood.

I dropped in at Baker Street a few times, uninvited. He was pleased to see me, I think, but it was painful for both of us to find ourselves alone together on the old shared territory; and he could never resist rubbing salt in the wound by remarking how wedlock suited me, how much weight I had put on, how thriving was my appearance, and so on.

As time passed, we saw one another less and less frequently. He engrossed himself in his work; since my published accounts of his cases had made him well known, he was much sought after. I knew that his cocaine habit had an increased hold over him, and that there was nothing I could do or say to dissuade him from it. At the conclusion of the Sholto affair, I had made a rather tasteless remark to the effect that I had done better out of the case than he, since I had gained a wife, and he not even the proper recognition for all his work, as the credit was likely to go to Athelney Jones.

'There still remains the cocaine bottle,' was all that Holmes had said.

I understand now what I could not then perceive, that he used the drug to deaden the turmoil within him, and that my marriage increased that turmoil. But my instinct at the time was one of self-preservation, and since my love for him made life at Baker Street a torment to me, I grasped the lucky chance that had come my way, and left him to the tender mercies of the drug.

I was startled out of my reverie by the entrance of the maid announcing that the first patient of the day had arrived. I had not even heard the doorbell. Hastily I removed my dressing gown, donned my frock-coat, and made my way to my consulting room. For the next few hours at least, I must put Sherlock Holmes out of my mind.

'Well, here is the train already,' said Mary as we approached the platform. 'I might as well get on and find myself a good seat. You don't have to wait.'

'I would like to wave you off,' I said.

I missed her when she was away, and it always surprised me. Sometimes I wondered whether she missed me when I disappeared in answer to a summons from Holmes. If she did, she never showed it.

We approached the ladies' carriage, and she was pleased to find it uncrowded.

'I shall probably travel back on the Sunday,' she said. 'It will be quieter. Unless you hear otherwise, you may expect me in time for dinner.'

I nodded. 'Do give my regards to Mrs Forrester. I hope you find her well.'

'So do I. Do you know, it has been three months . . . a long time. I feel unaccountably nervous.'

I laughed. Nervousness was not a quality that I could ever associate with Mary. 'Will there . . . be other guests?'

'Not at first, I hope. But if I should encounter Anne D'Arcy, I will be sure to remember you to her.'

'Please do.' I was aware that a mutual wariness existed between my wife and Miss D'Arcy, and that Mrs Forrester was the cause of it; but I never enquired too deeply into the complications of their circle. To be honest, even after three years of mutual domesticity, I found Mary's private life somewhat disturbing to contemplate;

which was unreasonable in me, as she was perfectly sanguine about mine.

Mary boarded the train, and I assisted her with her portmanteaux. She settled herself at a window seat, and we continued our conversation through the open window.

'Anyway, John, James, or whatever you call yourself, be sure to keep well, and be discreet, there's a good boy.'

'I am always discreet,' I said, somewhat huffily.

'My dear husband, you are not. But far be it from me to lecture you. Just don't shock the servants; and if you should by any chance be whisked away, do just pause to send me a wire. If I return to an empty house and find that I could have prolonged my visit, I shall be most annoyed.'

'Prolong your visit anyway, my dear, if you wish; but I do not anticipate being whisked away. I shall certainly be in touch if anything untoward occurs.'

The final slamming of doors and the shrill of the guard's whistle proclaimed that the train was about to depart. Mary hastily leaned out of the window and kissed me on both cheeks.

'Have fun,' she said.

'And you.'

I felt no premonition, no twinge of foreboding; but the ground was to shift from under my feet before I saw her again.

## — *II* —

I WAS READING quietly in my consulting room that evening, when I heard the clang of the doorbell. The maid went to answer it, and I paused in mid-sentence to listen, fervently hoping it was not a late call on my professional services.

My heart leapt wildly as I caught the strains of his voice. A moment later, Sherlock Holmes was standing before me.

For a few seconds we looked at one another without speaking. I searched his face; he was even paler and thinner than usual. There were deep shallows under his eyes, and his expression was one of harassed anxiety. His dark hair, usually smoothed back so meticulously, was dishevelled. He smoothed it hurriedly with his hands and gave a quick, rueful smile.

'Yes, I have been using myself up rather too freely,' he said.

I opened my lips to speak, and hesitated. My concern for his health was evident; it was not the way to greet him.

'I . . . thought you were in France,' I said instead. I took in his thin frame, his tense posture. 'I received your letters,' I added.

He did not reply, but turned to the window. 'Have you any objection to my closing your shutters?' he said in a clipped, strained voice.

I looked from him to the window in alarm.

'Why . . . no,' I said, 'but — ' I stopped in mid-sentence as he darted to the wall, edged his way round it to the window, and flinging the shutters together, bolted them securely. Such behaviour was so utterly unexpected that it produced a knot of fear in my solar plexus.

'You are afraid of something?' I said.

'Well, I am.'

'Of what?'

'Of air-guns.'

By now I was seriously alarmed for his state of mind. It must have showed in my face, for he smiled and shook his head as if to reassure me.

'I think you know me well enough, Watson, to understand that I am not usually the nervous type. But it is stupidity rather than courage to refuse to recognise danger when it is close upon you.'

He appeared to make an effort to calm himself. He sat down in the armchair beside my desk and took out his old silver cigarette case.

'May I trouble you for a match?'

I lit his cigarette for him. Our eyes met as he leaned towards me.

'I must apologise for calling so late,' he said, drawing in the smoke gratefully. I had never seen him so nervous.

'You always arrive at unconventional hours.' I tried an unsteady laugh.

'I shall have to leave in an even more unconventional manner, over your back garden wall.'

I gaped. 'Holmes, what is all this?' I said quickly.

He held out his hand, and I saw in the light of the lamp that two of his knuckles were burst and bleeding.

'Oh God, how did that happen?' I tried to take his hand, but he withdrew it.

'It's not an airy nothing, you see,' said he, smiling. 'Is Mrs Watson in?'

'She is away on a visit,' I said impatiently.

'Indeed! You are alone?'

'Quite. You knew I was alone, Holmes, or you would never have come.'

He looked at me reproachfully, and ignored the comment.

'Then it makes it the easier for me to propose that you should come away with me for a week, on the Continent.'

I stared. I could not keep pace with him. I looked around for my own cigarettes, and he offered me his case. His eyes remained fixed on my face as he waited for an answer.

'Where?' I said softly.

'Oh anywhere. It's all the same to me.'

I was nonplussed and shaken. I looked again at the blood on his hand. 'What case is this?' I said. 'And your hand — what happened? Tell me.'

Holmes took a deep breath and stubbed out his cigarette. He leaned forward with his elbows upon his knees, fingertips together. 'Have you ever heard of Professor Moriarty?' he said.

'Never,' I replied absently, looking at the pallor of his thin hands in the lamplight.

'Yes you have, Watson,' he said impatiently. 'You remember the Vermissa Valley business.'

'Ah yes. I'm sorry,' I said, trying to pull myself together. 'He was the mastermind behind the hounding of Jack Douglas.'

'That's right. You remember how I described him then.'

'You described him as a scientific genius.'

I did indeed remember that Holmes had been somewhat effusive upon the subject of Professor Moriarty. He appeared to see in him the old medieval ideal of the worthy opponent. Inspector Macdonald had let slip that it was the opinion of the official force that my friend had something of 'a bee in his bonnet' about the man; and I could not help leaning towards the same opinion myself. However, over the last few years, certainly since my marriage, I had not heard Holmes so much as mention his name. I had presumed that Moriarty, like so many master criminals before him, had faded into respectable retirement; or maybe had come to a sticky and ignominious end. I was somewhat alarmed, therefore, to hear his name once more on my friend's lips, and my alarm deepened as I listened to the tale he told me that evening.

He described Moriarty as the 'Napoleon of Crime'. He said that he was the organiser of half that was evil and of nearly all that was undetected in the City of London, but that he was fenced round with safeguards so cunningly devised that it seemed impossible to get evidence that would convict him in a court of law. He explained that for the last few months he, Holmes, had been trying to weave a net round him that would haul him in and send his whole criminal empire crashing to the ground.

'You know my powers, my dear Watson,' he said. 'And yet at the end of three months I was forced to confess that I had at last met an antagonist who was my intellectual equal.'

He told me that Moriarty had paid him an unexpected visit that morning, in an attempt to dissuade him from his efforts, and gave me a verbatim account of their conversation, which seemed chiefly to consist of compliments upon one another's genius, and mutual assurances that every argument they could use against one another had already crossed both their minds.

I must admit that I experienced an unpleasant pang of jealousy over my friend's obvious fascination with the man, which his assurances of his evil disposition and physical ugliness did little to dispel. For months, then, when my mind had been filled only with thoughts of him, his had been filled with Moriarty.

'I tell you, Watson, in all seriousness,' he said, 'that if I could beat the man, if I could free society of him, I should feel that my own career had reached its summit, and I should be prepared to turn to some more placid line in life.'

He would never have taken such a step for my sake, I thought.

At last, as he talked, I was able to piece together the reason for his visit and his unexpected proposal.

Apparently it was now only a matter of three days before Moriarty and all his gang would be in the hands of the police, thanks to Holmes' efforts; and for this reason, Moriarty was determined to put him out of action, permanently if possible. This was the story behind his bleeding hand. Already he had been attacked three times: once by a furiously driven two-horse van which had narrowly missed him; once by a brick which fell as if by accident from one of the houses in Vere Street and shattered to fragments at his feet; and once, on his way to me, by a rough with a bludgeon, upon whose front teeth he had barked his knuckles. He had spent most of the day in the safety of his brother Mycroft's club in Pall Mall.

Of course, I was horrified to hear of the danger he was in, and implored him to spend the night under my roof.

'You cannot go back to Baker Street,' I said. 'Stay here with me. I promise you will be quite safe. Please, Holmes. I shall not get a wink of sleep for worrying about you, if you go.'

'No, Watson. You would find me a dangerous guest.'

'Do you think that that weighs with me for an instant?'

'No, my dear Watson, but it weighs with me. Listen, will you come with me tomorrow? Can you start tomorrow morning? I must get you over to the Continent.'

'Why certainly I can, but can't you — ' I stopped short. The import of his last words had suddenly struck me. 'What do you mean, you must get me over to the Continent?'

Holmes slowly lit another cigarette, and eyed me quizzically. I watched him in an agony of impatience. 'What do you mean?' I repeated.

'If it were just my own safety that I was worried about,' he said at last, very quietly, 'I would have placed myself in police custody until after the trial, and not even contacted you until all was over. But I am afraid, my dear friend, that things are a little more complicated than that. Moriaty's powers of observation and investigation are quite equal to my own. Just as I know the names, occupations and personal habits of his confederates, so he is conversant with those of mine; and he made it quite clear, in this morning's conversation, that he would not hesitate to get at me through you.

' "If you are clever enough to bring destruction upon me," he said, "rest assured that I shall do as much to you."

' "You have paid me several compliments, Mr Moriarty," said I. "Let me pay you one in return, when I say that if I were assured of the former eventuality I would, in the interests of the public, cheerfully accept the latter."

' "Of course, you put the interests of the public above those of your friend?" he said very softly. I affected not to know what he meant, and raised my eyebrows. "I have, as you know, reliable contacts in all walks of life," he continued calmly, "and among them are several who, if put into the witness box as you intend, could easily be prevailed upon to name names in the course of their evidence; and I must warn you, Mr Holmes, that your friend Dr Watson will certainly be among them. I fear he has not been over discreet of late; it is a great shame. Such a thriving practice; such an understanding wife; and all to no purpose."

'He gave a slow, hideous smile as he spoke these words, Watson. I pretended to be unmoved. I repeated, with a great show of conviction, that I was determined to destroy him at any price. He snarled at me, and left.

'Of course, there are some prices which will always be too high, and I have every intention that you should be out of the country when this trial takes place. We can assess the damage in retrospect, and act accordingly. But you must come away tomorrow.'

I heard him in stunned silence. The emotions which agitated in my breast must have been reflected in rapid succession in my face; the shock of knowing that my movements were watched, the shame that my indiscretions had been brought to Holmes' notice in this way, the fear for my reputation and Mary's security; none of them could eclipse the joy of knowing that even to destroy the Napoleon of Crime, my friend would not put me in danger.

My throat was so dry as to make speech impossible. I ran my tongue over my lips to moisten them, and felt them to be as cold as ice. Holmes watched me gravely.

'You see what has come of your incautious behaviour, my dear fellow,' he said gently. In spite of everything, I thought I detected a note of pleasure in his voice; pleasure at having shaken the independence and security which he had resented in me for so long.

'But I do not see how — who are these people, these witnesses?' I found a voice at last, albeit a high and unsteady one.

'You must begin to appreciate the scope of the man's organisation,' said Holmes patiently. 'Wherever there is organised crime — or organised vice — there is the hand of Moriarty. I have met several of his contacts in that area myself during the course of my investigations; young boys, many of them, who are only trying to save themselves from starvation; or soldiers seeking to supplement their meagre pay. Ah! So that is it. I can read it in your face, Watson. I hope you have not been seen in public — '

'No,' I said quickly. But I shuddered inwardly, remembering yesterday's invitation to luncheon. I had always assumed that soldiers, whose own positions were so vulnerable, were fairly safe companions. I shuddered again at the magnitude of my mistake.

'My dear fellow, you need a brandy; your nerves are all in shreds. No, not for me. I must be going. Take some yourself when I have left, and be sure to stay calm and collected. Now listen. Here are your instructions for tomorrow, and I beg, my dear Watson, that you will obey them to the letter, for you are now playing a double-handed game with me against the cleverest rogue and the most powerful syndicate of criminals in Europe. Now listen! You will dispatch whatever luggage you intend to take by a trusty messenger unaddressed to Victoria tonight . . .'

He went on to issue a most complicated set of instructions, which led to a rendezvous in the second first-class carriage from the front of the Continental express at Victoria Station the next morning. He made me repeat them several times, and even insisted that I take notes, judging no doubt my dazed and shocked state to be a hindrance to an accurate memory. Mechanically I repeated the whole bizarre arrangement and assured him that I understood and would comply.

'I must send a wire to Mary,' I said.

He shook his head urgently. 'No. Not yet. Wire her tomorrow from the Continent. We cannot run the risk of its being intercepted.'

'Very well,' I acquiesced. I had not thought of that.

It was in vain that I pleaded with him to remain for the night. It was evident that his fears for me as well as for himself were the motive which compelled him to go. After a few more words he rose and came out with me into the garden, clambering over the wall which led into Mortimer Street, and immediately whistling for a hansom, in which I heard him drive away.

## — *III* —

I HAVE WRITTEN elsewhere of the complicated sequence of events which led up to our sojourn on the Continent and our eventual arrival at the little village of Meiringen on the 3rd of May, and I do not intend to repeat myself here; the purpose of this account is not to reiterate what has already been said, but to supplement it with what I was forced, at the time, to leave unsaid.

I will therefore state here very briefly that we sailed for the Continent, not from Dover as we had intended, but from Newhaven, having abandoned our scheduled train, and our luggage with it, at Canterbury to put Moriarty off our trail. Accordingly we arrived, not at Paris as Moriarty anticipated, but at Dieppe, whence we made our way to Brussels.

There I despatched a telegram to Mary. I did not impart anything concerning the alarming circumstances of my departure; I merely stated: 'Have been whisked away to the Continent for a short holiday. Do prolong your visit if convenient. Will let you know how things progress. S.H. sends regards.' I deduced that, knowing whom I was with, she would be less likely to worry if my stay were prolonged or if there were any unexpected developments.

After two days in Brussels we moved on to Strasbourg. There

Holmes received a telegram informing him that Moriarty had slipped the net. The police had secured the whole gang with the exception of him. Holmes was furious.

'Of course, when I had left the country, there was no one left to cope with him,' he snapped, hurling the telegram into the grate, nuch to the astonishment of our fellow diners in the hotel *salle-à-manger*. 'But I did think I had put the game in their hands.'

I watched him anxiously, crumbling a piece of bread roll between my finger and thumb. He had been as tense as a coiled spring for the last three days, and I feared an extreme reaction.

'Where do you think he is?' I asked.

'On our trail. It will only be a matter of time before he catches up with me. And with you. I think that you had better return to England, Watson.'

'Why? I thought you wanted me to stay here until after the trial. I thought you said I would be safer over here.'

'And so you would, if Moriarty were in police custody. Then his only channel of revenge would be the attempted ruin of your reputation from the witness box. As it is, however, he is after bigger fish; he will devote his whole energies to revenging himself on me. He said as much in our short interview, and I fancy he meant it. I think, my dear friend, that you would be safer away from my company.'

I stared at him across the table. He avoided my gaze.

'How could you think that I would leave you in danger?' I whispered.

Holmes looked sideways at the approaching waiter.

'Now Watson, be logical, there's a good fellow. Let us discuss this seriously over dinner. It looks as if they keep an excellent cellar here; what would you say to a bottle of Château Lafite?'

We argued the question over dinner for nearly two hours. I was determined that nothing would persuade me to leave him. I cannot for the life of me recall what we ate, but I vividly remember the mingled taste in my mouth of wine and panic. The claret was very red; I remember turning the thin stem of the glass in my hand. Holmes was logical and gentle; he did not try to bully me. I think — I am sure — that my devotion touched him, in spite of himself. He said that he regretted ever having involved me in the business; he said that he would have me on his conscience if I did not leave for England immediately; that my presence would in any case hinder him from achieving the only goal left to him. But I remained adamant, and the same night we had resumed our journey and were well on the way to Geneva. There was a fanatical look in his eyes, however, and an edge to his voice when he spoke of 'the only goal left to him', which disturbed me more than his danger, or mine.

I need hardly say that I will never forget the week we spent wandering up the valley of the Rhone, over the Gemmi Pass and on through Interlaken. 'A charming week', I think I called it in my published account. The beauty of our surroundings made an idyllic setting for a leisurely walking holiday; the little hotels that we patronised were clean, friendly and discreet. How often had I dreamed of such a week with Holmes, such leisure, such privacy, such scenery. We wandered among vineyards and orchards, with the slopes of the mountain rising almost sheer above us, the snow-capped heights dappled with sunlight and shadow as the clouds moved over across the sky. In the evenings we would dine quietly, usually in a small hotel *salle-à-manger* overlooking the river. At night we would lie awake and talk into the small hours; in the morning we would breakfast on coffee and hot croissants, and then set off once more into the fresh delight of a spring day. I was of course painfully aware that the circumstances were far from ideal; and Holmes' constant references to the fact that he would cheerfully bring his career to a conclusion, if he could be assured that society was free of Professor Moriarty, both alarmed and puzzled me. Behind his single-minded eagerness I sensed an element of self-destruction.

I tried to make light of his obsession and to encourage him to do the same. 'You are so vain, Holmes,' I remarked one night, when he had concluded a little speech to the effect that the air of London was the sweeter for his presence, and that if his record were closed that night he would be able to survey it with equanimity. 'I think you have a tendency to view yourself in an almost Messianic light. You just want to go out in a blaze of glory. What good will that do for us ordinary mortals? You seem to think that Moriarty is unique, but I would be willing to wager that his chair will not remain vacant for so very long; and then, shy and self-effacing as you are, I think you would be coaxed out of retirement with very little persuasion.'

I spoke into the darkness, gazing up at the faint pallor of the ceiling. I heard the creak of his bedsprings as he made a quick, annoyed movement, and turning my head could dimly see his outline, propped upon one elbow, looking across at me.

'You refuse to grasp the reality of the situation, Watson,' he said. 'Moriarty is unique, because of his genius.'

'Ah yes, a genius that is matched only by your own. You *are* vain,

Holmes.'

'I am not vain,' he snapped. 'I am merely stating the facts. There is no virtue in false modesty, Watson. I know that I am the only man alive who can match him. I am being quite truthful when I say that to overcome him would be the pinnacle of my career; and that I would count not only my career, but my life well spent in the process.'

I felt my throat constrict.

'Don't be ridiculous, Holmes. Supposing you were to lose your life and he to keep his? You said he was your equal. There is no need to take senseless risks.'

'But for the good of society, Watson. And there are always risks.'

'Society can go to hell,' I said with a ferocity that surprised us both. 'This is a personal contest between you and him, and you couldn't care less what happens to society or to — anyone else. You are just obsessed with the need to best him. It's transparent.'

'Absolute rubbish, Watson,' he snapped, and turned away from me, pulling the sheets up over his ears. I stared, as I often stared, across the space between our two beds, at the outline of the hump he made under the blankets and the shock of black hair upon the pillow; and took several deep breaths to calm myself.

'Holmes, can't you grasp the simple fact that I fear for your safety?' I said as steadily as I could into the darkness.

'I am quite capable of looking after myself,' came the muffled, dignified reply.

'No, you are not. You are under too much mental strain. You are not well, Holmes. I can see it. You are just in the state to throw yourself into unnecessary danger.'

'Don't try to nursemaid me, Doctor. I can assure you that I neither need nor want it.'

The words hung between us in the silence that followed. I spoke again as soon as I could.

'I need you, though. Don't you ever think about me, Holmes? Or has Moriarty eclipsed everything?'

I heard him turn over. I remained staring at the ceiling.

'You don't need me, Watson. You are doing perfectly well without me.'

After the briefest of pauses, I said quietly, 'What makes you think that?'

'I deduce it,' he said, 'from your style of living.'

'What do you mean?'

He did not reply. His silence made me angry.

'You know perfectly well,' I said bitterly, 'that I married for convenience, and to protect your reputation as well as mine.'

'My reputation can speak for itself, thank you.'

I sat up angrily in bed and turned towards him. I spoke clearly and painfully into the space between us.

'All right, then,' I said, 'I married to protect you from me. Is that satisfactory? I married because I could not go on as we were. And you act as if I deserted you unreasonably. You talk as if I were wallowing in domestic bliss. You are surely aware that Mary and I enjoy a purely friendly relationship. Is that the way of life that you so much object to? Do you deduce from this that I have no need for your friendship?'

I waited, counting the seconds. Not since before my marriage had I spoken so frankly. His reply, when it came, took me completely by surprise.

'I was not referring,' he said, 'to your marriage.'

I let myself fall back onto the pillow, and lay quite still. I felt the room spin in the darkness. It was a long time before I could think of anything to say.

'You are mad,' I said at last.

'On the contrary, it is a perfectly logical deduction.'

'You think that I keep other company because I prefer it to yours?'

'I think that you have chosen according to your priorities.'

I gasped and turned to look at him once more. He was still staring at the ceiling.

'And what incentive can you offer me, to change this way of living that you despise so much? Do you think that your own is any more healthy? Cocaine, ambition, obsession?'

He was silent for a moment, and then said quietly, 'You ask the impossible.'

'And so do you!'

I turned my face away from him. My cheek was wet against the pillow. His selfishness, his childishness overwhelmed me. His twisting of the facts convinced me that he was in an unbalanced and paranoid state of mind. I heard him settle down to sleep. There was nothing more to say, it seemed. All the same, I had to have the last word.

'I don't know why we continue to torture each other,' I said. 'I sometimes think that it would be better if we never saw each other again.'

There was no reply, only the steady sound of his breathing. It was too late to bite out my tongue.

# — IV —

THE NEXT MORNING found me sluggish and dazed. Neither of us referred to the conversation of the night before. I tried to indicate by my penitent and solicitous manner that I was sorry for what I had said, but he was angry and this made it difficult. I watched helplessly as he reached into the inner recesses of his coat and extracted his morocco case and cocaine bottle. Deftly he rolled back his left sleeve and I saw the puncture marks which scarred the white skin of his arm. I wondered vaguely how much cocaine he had brought with him, and what he would do if we were far from a druggist when it ran out.

That day we crossed over the Gemmi Pass. For this we needed a guide, and his presence made it even more difficult for me to apologise to Holmes, or to ask him to speak further of the resentment he had betrayed, which I still thought to be unreasonable. I brooded silently on the matter as we walked in single file along the narrow pathway. To our right was the steep, dangerous incline of the mountain; the grey-green of the moss and the short, tufty grass, the gleaming slabs of bare rock, relieved by dustings of small, star-like flowers. To our left was a steep drop to the green waters of the melancholy Daubensee. The sun shone thinly and the air was cold. I kept my eyes fixed on the path and mentally rehearsed our angry exchange and its implications.

Surely it was insane and cruel of Holmes to apply his own standards of behaviour to me in the very area in which he himself was confused, defensive and frigid; how could he expect me to live in self-imposed celibacy just because he did? When he knew that I loved him, and that it was his decree that forbade me from expressing that love? However, I could not avoid the knowledge that things might seem different from his point of view; that he saw me as undisciplined, self-indulgent, placing the pleasures of the flesh above the ties of friendship, leaving him in favour of a life of reckless hedonism because he had refused me one thing. It was an unpleasant thought, and I tried to reason it away. But it had taken root, had implanted itself in the wall of my mind, and I could not get rid of it.

Suddenly there was a loud rumble above us, and we all three instinctively lurched forward just in time to avoid a large rock which had been dislodged from the ridge upon our right. It clattered down and roared into the lake behind us. In an instant Holmes had raced up on to the ridge, and, standing upon a lofty pinnacle, craned his neck in every direction. It was in vain that our guide assured him that a fall of stones was a common chance in springtime at that spot. He descended the slope and gave me a slow, grim smile, as if to say that this was nothing more than the fulfilment of what he had expected.

I scanned the ridge with anxious eyes but could see nothing. I did not know what to believe; the guide was insistent, and Holmes was undoubtedly paranoid. And yet — if Moriarty were indeed on our trail, he could well have caught up with us by now. I turned back to Holmes with a questioning expression, and opened my mouth to speak; but he shook his head quickly to silence me, and we resumed our journey.

It was a fatal mixture of pride and humility which prevented me from referring to our argument again. I was thinking the matter over; and did not want to offer any apologies or promises until my own mind was clearer on the subject. Holmes meanwhile appeared to recover his equanimity, though he spoke less on the subject of Moriarty, and brooded more. His words, expression and actions all took on a determined quality which was in itself a defence against intrusion on my part.

On the 3rd of May, we reached the little village of Meiringen, where we put up at the Englischer Hof, then kept by Peter Steiler the elder; a large, jovial man who spoke excellent English, having served for three years as waiter at the Grosvenor Hotel in London. He appeared to take a liking to us, and joined us at our table after dinner when the few other guests had retired, insisting that we accept his offer of liqueurs on the house. Holmes, usually so morose in uninvited company (unless it were a client), appeared to be in an excellent mood, and regaled our host with tales of London, even managing to exhume a mutual acquaintance or two. The easy, humorous atmosphere was infectious, and I was on the point of naming an acquaintance or two of my own in connection with the Grosvenor, when Holmes abruptly changed the subject.

'So, we are your first English visitors of the season?' he enquired of Steiler, offering him a cigarette from his silver case, which the latter accepted with pleasure.

'The first, yes. But in the summer usually we have many English here. Ah, Herr Holmes, you should see how busy is my little hotel in the summer! But the spring is nicer for you. Not so crowded. Two gentlemen like yourself and the Doctor do not wish to be crowded. And you will see, the falls of Reichenbach are so beautiful in the spring. So — majestic, Herr Holmes, and solemn also. But beauty!

Ah, you must certainly go, and yourself, Dr Watson, it is a sight not to be missed! In the summer, they all come for it.'

'Well, yes, we shall certainly take a look at the Falls, eh Watson? Perhaps we can make a little detour, en route to Rosenlaui tomorrow.'

'Tomorrow? You go to Rosenlaui tomorrow?' Herr Steiler seemed quite upset at the thought. 'Ah, it is much too soon, you do not have the time to relax and enjoy our charming village. You will stay here, rest, it is so quiet, much rest and privacy for you both, you will enjoy much better.'

I regarded our host with some alarm. It was becoming increasingly obvious that he imagined us to be indulging in some sort of romantic idyll; he winked at me as he poured yet another measure of his clear, scented and extremely potent liqueur into my unresisting glass. Already flushed with alcohol, I felt my cheeks grow even hotter, and cast a look of helpless appeal at Holmes. The smile remained on his lips, but not in his eyes. He refused to meet my gaze.

'Indeed, you are most kind and persuasive, Herr Steiler,' he said, in sweet, icy tones. 'But I fear we must keep to our plans. There is so much of your beautiful country to see, and time, alas, is pressing.'

Herr Steiler, by now much the worse for drink, seemed totally oblivious to the warning note in my friend's voice. Heartily and fulsomely he expressed his regret, and turned his attention back to the subject of the Grosvenor and, unfortunately, to me. He obviously felt that he had neglected me during the earlier part of the conversation, and attempted to make up for it now by a barrage of questions and innuendos with which I felt totally unable to deal. He mentioned people I knew, and seeing me blush, he actually leaned over and pinched my arm. From the corner of my eye, I thought I saw Holmes flinch, but any comfort I might have derived from that reaction was drowned in my confusion. I tried to laugh the matter off, and claimed to be too tired and too much the worse for wine, to be able to embark on any reminiscences. Holmes had pushed his liqueur away from him, and sat leaning back in his chair, regarding us both with a cool, sardonic gaze that made me feel quite sick with anxiety.

Eventually he appeared to take pity on me, and proclaimed that it really was time for us to retire. He bade Herr Steiler a polite farewell and thanked him for his hospitality.

The room which our host had allotted us was furnished in heavy oak, and boasted of one large bedstead placed conspicuously in the middle of it.

I regarded it with dismay, but Holmes seemed completely unmoved. He removed his coat, laid it on the bed and began to rummage for his cocaine. I sat down upon the hard mattress and gazed at him unhappily.

'I'm sorry, Holmes,' I said.

'Sorry for what, my dear fellow? It was not your fault. It was a misunderstanding on the part of Herr Steiler.'

He placed his morocco case and bottle on the counterpane and avoided my eye. His voice was calm but I sensed anger in every syllable.

'But why—?' I faltered, and swallowed hard. 'I don't understand how he could have gained such an impression.'

'Appearances, my dear Watson,' said Holmes briefly.

I watched him fill his syringe and inject. He was sickened by the whole situation, I could see. Sickened that a man like Steiler, recognising me for what I was, should make the same assumptions about him. Sickened by my way of life and all that it represented. Sickened by me.

I sat silent, frozen with horror. I felt him turn to look at me.

'Go to bed, Watson,' he said gently. 'You'll feel better in the morning.'

Carefully he replaced the syringe in its case and stowed it away with the bottle. He rose from the bed and went to turn off the gas. He yawned and stretched like a cat, with animal grace, silhouetted against the window in his waistcoat and shirtsleeves. Moonlight streamed around him, onto the bed.

'Aren't you . . . going to sleep?' I asked.

He ran a hand through his black hair, and half turned towards me.

'I'm not tired. I'll sit up for a bit. It's a beautiful night, and I need time to think.' He picked up a chair from beside the dressing table and placed it by the window.

'Holmes,' I said, 'you don't have to sit up in that. I'll . . .'

He silenced me with an impatient gesture, and we both froze. There was an unmistakeable creak on the stair outside; then another; then a third, as someone crossed the landing. Swiftly and silently, Holmes crossed the room, and slid the bolt into place. We both listened. Someone was breathing heavily on the other side of the door. There was no doubt in my mind that it was Herr Steiler.

In the moonlight I could clearly see the anger and disgust on Holmes' face. He caught my glance and made a sign to me to get into bed. Then he crossed the room again and pulled the curtains to.

I undressed as noiselessly as I could in the darkness, got into bed and lay quite still. I heard a grunt of disappointment from the other side of the door, and the creak of the stairs as our voyeur retreated.

I turned my face to the window. My eyes had grown accustomed to the dark, and I could see Holmes sitting in the chair, his head bent forward and his fingertips together as though deep in concentration.

'He's gone, Holmes,' I whispered.

He grunted. 'Good night, Watson. Sleep well,' was all he said.

## — *V* —

I AWOKE IN the morning to find Holmes bending over a breakfast tray, pouring out coffee. The curtains were drawn, and sunlight and birdsong streamed through the window.

I blinked stupidly up at him as he held out a cup to me.

'Sit up and drink this, Watson,' he said. 'I took the precaution of going downstairs to fetch it myself. I explained to our host that I am an early riser. He said that we should have let him know when we wanted to be called and he would have brought the coffee himself. But it was too late, and I insisted. Here.'

I sat up in bed and sipped at the coffee. A glance at Holmes' face told me that he had hardly slept at all last night.

'Did you get any sleep?' I asked, all the same.

'A little. I feel perfectly refreshed. I suspect, from the colour of your eyes, that I feel better than you do, Watson.'

I put my hand up to my head. Herr Steiler's liqueurs were wreaking their revenge. I looked at the other half of the bed. It was undisturbed. He had slept in the chair, then. The room was heavy with the acrid smell of tobacco.

'You've been smoking all night again,' I said.

Holmes chuckled and went to fling open the window.

'There. Fresh air will soon clear the room and your head. Now, take time over your coffee and then come downstairs to breakfast. Mine host murmured something about the other guests breakfasting at nine, and I think it would be best if we did the same. I am just going for a brisk turn round the village.'

I did as I was told. It was a beautiful morning, and my fragile state made me particularly sensitive to its freshness and transparent quality; but there was coiled in my stomach a small worm of fear, which nuzzled and ate at my inner parts; and the unpleasant taste of last night's episode was in my mouth.

Holmes, too, seemed tense and worried; the shadows under his eyes gave him a look of one who is hunted; but his manner to me was particularly gentle, and he made no mention of the previous night.

I was glad when we eventually set off in the early afternoon, up the hill which led to the famous Reichenbach Falls. Herr Steiler bid us a tender farewell, and we were more than glad to say goodbye to him. We had arranged for our bags to be sent on to the hotel at Rosenlaui, to await us that evening. The walk over the hills was not too arduous, and we had plenty of time.

'It's a beautiful day, Holmes,' I said, making conversation as we climbed among the greens and yellows of the Alpine spring. The air was cool and seemed to glitter above and around us like crystal.

Holmes gave a small, tight smile. 'Beautiful,' he agreed; but his mind was elsewhere.

'Don't worry about Steiler,' I said timidly. 'We'll soon have him far behind, he can't do us any harm.'

Holmes sighed. 'I suppose not.'

I was sure now that the events of the previous evening still haunted him. I tried to sound sensible, to put things in perspective. 'At least there's no sign of Moriarty,' I said.

Holmes turned to me. 'You think not? On the contrary, I sense that he is very close. He will catch up with us within the next few days. He will give our descriptions to Herr Steiler and trace us easily.'

To my surprise he slowed and stopped in his tracks. He stood still for a while, then turned aside and sat down heavily on a boulder. We had not gone far, and he was not usually the first to flag; but he had the look of one who is utterly exhausted. I went to sit beside him.

'Holmes, what is it?' I said gently. 'Have you heard something? Let me know what it is, for God's sake. You know I'll do anything I can to help. You don't trust Steiler, is that it? Well, even if he does let out that we've been here, we're no worse off than we were at every other hotel. What makes you think that Moriarty is so much closer today than he was yesterday?'

Holmes sat silently, his head bent. When he turned to look at me, there was such a tired, hopeless look in his eyes that my heart gave a lurch of fear.

'Nothing,' he answered. 'Nothing. But I sense it. It's not a logical deduction, I know. But I wish — I wish it were all over and done with, Watson. I just wish I could get it all over. I must have some peace,' he added in a very low voice.

I was alarmed. It was as if the thread which had been taut inside him, drawing him on, his obsession with Moriarty and his determination to get the better of him, had suddenly snapped. As if the very bricks and mortar with which he had painstakingly built up his own personality were beginning to crumble; as if he had at last seen through what he had always believed to be his certainties, and found beyond them nothing but a grey and formless mist.

I said quietly, 'What is it that you wish was over and done with? Are you sure it is just Moriarty? Holmes, you know you don't have to put yourself through this; there is no reason why it has to come to a personal contest between you and him. Would it not be more sensible to return to England, where you will have the protection of the law and the police? There is no need to worry about me. Even if my name does come up in some way, it can all be dealt with; it has been done before, by people far more eminent than I. Just forget that side of it; come back to England with me, and let the police deal with Moriarty. I think you have come to the end of your tether. You need rest and — a change. A proper holiday. Holmes, I will do anything to help you; I would even — I would do anything.'

He was not listening to the last few words of my speech. He had raised his eyes and was gazing down the slope to the little village we had just left. The houses, the streets were tiny; it looked like a doll's village. Three figures were walking up the main street to the hotel. I imagined that I could reach down and pick one of them up between my thumb and forefinger.

' — end of my tether,' he murmured. 'Ha! Dead end of the road, and turn round and go back — it's not possible. I must have been right. I have to be right. It was the only thing to do. I couldn't be like that.'

I could not make sense of his mumbling, but it filled me with fear, and the small worm coiled in my stomach began to nuzzle again. I waited, in case he wanted to say more, but he lapsed into silence and stared fixedly and unblinkingly into space, twisting his Alpine-stock round and round in his hands.

At last I laid a hand upon his shoulder, and he jumped as if he had been stung or bitten.

'Holmes,' I said, hastily withdrawing my hand.

'Sorry, Watson.' He was on his feet. 'Must have fallen into a daydream. Come on, or we'll be too late to look at these Falls.'

I rose slowly, and we continued our climb. As we approached the Falls we became aware of the deep booming of the waters, echoing louder and louder, until it obliterated every trace of birdsong. The air became damp and green around us as we neared the place; the light was muted and took on an ominous, apocalyptic quality which added to our sense of awe.

It is, as I described in my published account, a fearful place. The torrent, swollen by the melting snow, plunges into a tremendous abyss, from which the spray rolls up like the smoke from a burning house. The shaft into which the river hurls itself is an immense chasm, lined by glistening, coal-black rock and narrowing into a creaming, boiling pit of incalculable depth, which brims over and shoots the stream onward over its jagged lip. The long sweep of green water, roaring forever down, and the thick flickering curtain of spray hissing forever upwards, turn one giddy with their constant whirl and clamour.

We walked along the path which reaches half-way round the edge of the abyss. It had been cut from the rock, to afford the observer a complete view, but it curtails abruptly in a dead end, and the traveller has to turn back and retrace his steps in order to continue his journey. Holmes and I stood for some time peering down at the gleam of the breaking water far below us against the black rocks, and listening to the half-human cry which came booming up with the spray out of the abyss. For a while, neither of us spoke. In my weak and frightened state, I found myself quite overcome by the force and majesty of the place; it impressed me with a sense of age — age far greater than mankind; with a sense of animal wilfulness and impartial caprice. It was the abode of the ancient gods of stone and water; it engulfed our petty human concerns and flung them down into its depths.

From beside me, I heard Holmes say quite clearly, 'So it makes no difference in the end, after all. Quite useless. It is intolerable.' How I managed to hear his quiet voice above the roar of the waters, I do not know. I do not think he meant me to hear.

'Come along, Holmes,' I said loudly, after a few minutes' further silence. 'Let us go back now.'

He looked at me blankly.

'It is a dead end,' I shouted above the spray. 'We have to turn back and find the path again.'

He looked about wildly, like one who has just woken from a dream, and then suddenly his gaze fixed upon something over my shoulder. I turned.

A figure was running towards us, along the path, waving something in his hand. We waited, frozen.

At last the boy reached us, red-faced and panting, holding out a folded piece of paper.

'Herr Doktor? Votson?' he said between gasps.

I stepped forward and took the paper. I unfolded it, and saw that it bore the mark of the Englischer Hof.

'What is this?' I said sharply.

'Ein Brief für Ihnen, Herr Doktor. Herr Steiler hat mir gesagt, dass ich Ihnen zurück bringen muss. Eine Dame, eine englische Dame, ist todkrank.'

I looked confusedly at the piece of paper.

'He says an English lady is dying,' translated Holmes unnecessarily, and leaned over my shoulder to read the letter with me.

It appeared to be from Herr Steiler himself. An English lady had arrived at the hotel, he said, within a few minutes of our leaving. She was in the last stages of consumption, and was travelling from Davos Platz, where she had wintered, to join her friends at Lucerne. A sudden haemorrhage had overtaken her. It was thought that she could only live a few hours. She was in great distress, asking to see an English doctor. She would not let the Swiss doctor go near her. Herr Steiler did not know what to do. If I would only return, just briefly, perhaps it would calm her. He would look on it as the greatest of favours. He had said that he would try to find an English doctor. Please would I do him this favour, for it was so great a responsibility — and so on.

Holmes and I stared at one another.

'Don't go,' he said. I stared at him in amazement.

'But I must! The lady is dying. Come with me.'

'No.'

'Come with me, Holmes. I don't want to leave you here. I must go to her; I can't refuse my services to a fellow countrywoman.'

We had walked back to the main path. The water roared behind us.

'I don't trust him,' said Holmes. 'How do you know this is not a trap?'

'Don't be ridiculous, Holmes. Why should it be? The poor lady must be desperate.'

'Moriarty is behind it.'

Once again, I stared at him. Surely this was proof of his unstable state of mind.

'How could he be?' I wailed over the din of the water. 'It is me they are asking for, not you. Look, I have to go, Holmes. I could not live with my conscience if I refused such a plea. You stay here, then, and wait for me. No — do not stay here' — for I had developed a nameless fear of the atmosphere of the place — 'go on to Rosenlaui. Take this boy with you . . . Will you — go on — with this gentleman — to Rosenlaui?' I shouted at the still breathless boy. He looked uncomprehendingly until I repeated the message with gestures, and then he seemed to understand and consent.

'Ja. Ja. Rosenlaui. Gehen wir darüber, mein Herr. Ist nicht so weit.'

He gestured to Holmes along the path. Holmes, whose German was far better than mine, did not offer to help at all with the conversation. He merely stood with folded arms, an indecipherable expression on his face. He made no effort to move.

'Please, Holmes,' I said desperately. I was torn between worry for him, in his present state of mind, and the call of duty. But I could honestly see no reason to take the message at anything but face value. If Moriarty were at the hotel, surely it would be Holmes he would try to lure, and not me? In my confusion, no other possibility occurred to me.

At last he shrugged, and nodded, as though he were past caring. He agreed to go on with the boy to Rosenlaui and wait for me there. I was sure to reach him by the evening. I told him we would have a good dinner.

He took out his watch and checked the time. He smiled, and suddenly clasped my hand.

'In Rosenlaui, then,' he said.

I returned the pressure of his hand, pleased to see him sensible at last, and set off down the road along which we had come. I said to myself that once we were safely installed at Rosenlaui, I would seriously set about persuading him to return to England. I would emphasise to him that I was truly alarmed for his health. I would try to be masterful and take charge of the situation. The idea rather appealed to me. And once back in England, I would see if it could not be arranged that I did not have to leave him so alone. I would speak to Mary. It would be difficult, very difficult, but surely something could be arranged? And if it were my companions rather than my marriage that he objected to, why then I would give up my companions. Good heavens, his friendship was more important to me than anything. If I had known before . . . if I had known that he minded, what might have happened? What might still be possible?

But no, that was dangerous and unnecessary. But I would speak to him about it. I would tell him that I understood, that I would change the way I lived. I would tell him this evening . . .

I turned back twice to look for him. The first time I saw him still standing with his back against a rock and his arms folded, gazing down at the rush of the waters. The second time I had descended too far to see either the Falls or Holmes, but I could see the curving path which wound over the shoulder of the hill. Along this path a man was walking very rapidly; I could see his black figure clearly outlined against the green behind him. I noted him, and the energy with which he walked, but he passed from my mind again as I hurried upon my errand.

It may have been a little over an hour before I reached Meiringen. Steiler was standing at the porch of his hotel. His face brightened when he saw me, and he came forward to meet me.

'Why, Dr Watson,' he said, 'what is this? Where is Herr Holmes?'

'Well, I trust she is no worse?' I was saying simultaneously.

We both stared at one another in surprise. At the first quiver of his eyebrows my heart turned to lead in my breast. I pulled the letter from my pocket and held it out to him with a trembling hand.

'You did not write this? There is no sick Englishwoman in the hotel?'

'Certainly not.'

He took the letter and glanced at it. 'But it has the hotel mark upon it!' he said slowly. He looked up at me in consternation. I caught an uneasy look in his eyes. 'The tall Englishman who came in after you had gone,' he said. 'He must have written it. He said —'

I did not wait to hear what he had said. The explanations could wait. I ran, in a tingle of fear, back to the path which I had just descended.

To run uphill, in fear and anxiety, when one is already exhausted, is not an experience I would wish on anyone. Several times I saw a red curtain shimmering before my eyes, and thought that my heart would burst, and shooting pains stabbed at my weak leg like red-hot needles. But the urgency, the absolute necessity of reaching Holmes before it was too late, drove me on beyond what would normally have been physically possible. It took me twice as long to run back to the Falls as it had taken me to run down.

I have described elsewhere what I found there.

Holmes' Alpine-stock was still leaning against the rock by which I had left him. At the end of the man-made ledge, where the path dovetailed into the sheer rock above the abyss, two lines of footmarks ended in a ploughed mass of mud, fringed with torn ferns and brambles; and the water plunged endlessly down, with its half-human cry and echo absorbing my frenzied shouts.

I found, upon the boulder by his Alpine-stock, his silver cigarette case and a note, which I once again will reproduce in full:

> My dear Watson,
>
> I write these lines through the courtesy of Mr Moriarty, who awaits my convenience for the final discussion of those questions which lie between us. He has been giving me a sketch of the methods by which he avoided the English police and kept himself informed of our movements. They certainly confirm the very high opinion which I had formed of his abilities. I am pleased to think that I shall be able to free society from any further effects of his presence, though I fear that it is at a cost which will give pain to my friends, and especially, my dear Watson, to you. I have already explained to you, however, that my career had in any case reached its crisis, and that no possible conclusion could be more congenial to me than this. Indeed, if I may make a full confession to you, I was quite convinced that the letter from Meiringen was a hoax, and I allowed you to depart on that errand under the persuasion that some development of this sort would follow. Tell Inspector Patterson that the papers which he needs to convict the gang are in pigeon-hole M, done up in a blue envelope and inscribed 'Moriarty'. I made every disposition of my property before I left England, and handed it to my brother Mycroft. Pray give my greetings to Mrs Watson, and believe me to be, my dear fellow,
>
> Very sincerely yours,
> Sherlock Holmes.

I read the note again and again. The handwriting was meticulous, and unmistakeably his. But what on earth had he meant by it? Even given that Moriarty were waiting as he wrote it, I could not believe that these were his last words to me.

Saying he feared to give pain to his friends — what friends? He knew there was only me. 'Making full confession' that he knew the note from Meiringen was a hoax, when he had asked me at once, oh

God, not to go. Instructions issued to Inspector Patterson, his odious brother named as his executor, greetings to 'Mrs Watson' — asking me to believe him to be very sincerely mine — dear heaven, it was impossible, it had to be impossible.

And yet, what other explanation was there? Never in a million years could I believe that he would pay so cruel a trick. It must be as the note said, Moriarty had caught him, he had given him but a few minutes to write, he had threatened him, menaced him, for there were no returning footprints. They had fallen together, locked in a deadly embrace. It was unthinkable — my imagination shrank from it.

I do not know how long I stood there; how many times I read the note; how often I ran to the edge of the path, threw myself down into the mud and howled into the torrent of the waters. I know that eventually I found myself running at full tilt back down the hill to Meiringen; that I collapsed into the arms of Herr Steiler and screamed filthy imprecations at him; that I had to be restrained by two Swiss policemen who eventually supported me along the path when I insisted on returning to the spot with the search party; that a wire was despatched to Rosenlaui and it was confirmed that though our baggage had arrived at the hotel, Holmes had not; that it was late in the evening when we had returned, and the path was bathed in moonlight; and that the Swiss physician was called to attend me, and to administer a sedative, while the grim, blond policeman took down my incoherent statement about Professor Moriarty.

## — *VI* —

IT WAS LATE in the morning when I woke. It was an awakening such as the human heart, I think, is ill-constructed to bear. There was sunlight and birdsong all around me, and an empty chair still stood by the open window. Herr Steiler himself, accompanied by the Swiss doctor, brought me coffee.

A team of experts had been back to the Falls, and their examination had left little doubt that a personal contest between the two men ended, as it could hardly fail to end in such a situation, in their reeling over, locked in each other's arms. Any attempt at recovering their bodies was regarded as hopeless, although an exploration party had been sent down, for form's sake. Their report, when it came, was negative as expected. There was no sign of the boy who had brought me the fatal letter; he seemed simply to have disappeared into thin air. Obviously he had been in the pay of Moriarty. Nor was there any trace of the two companions who, according to Herr Steiler, had arrived at the hotel with the 'tall Englishman'.

Herr Steiler was very kind. I felt sorry, by the time I left him, for the things I had screamed at him in my first shock. He arranged for the return of our baggage from Rosenlaui and for its transportation to England. He helped me to send the necessary telegrams. He was firm with the Swiss police, and did not allow them to interview me for too long.

He was, after all, the only person who had the least inkling of what I was suffering.

Moriarty and his companions, he confessed to me when I was in a more rational frame of mind and ready to leave for England, had made only the most innocent of enquiries; about the number of visitors at that time of year, and how long they usually stayed, and what brought them to Meiringen. Steiler had mentioned the Falls with pride, as he always did, and had said that he had advised two visitors only that afternoon to view them on their way to Rosenlaui. He had not even mentioned our nationality. There was no way he could have possibly suspected.

In the end, I was sorry to leave him, and the thought of London made me sick with dread.

My first six months back in London, before I fell ill, remain shrouded in mist; certain episodes flare out in my memory, cruel flashes of lucidity, but strangely I do not remember them in the order in which common sense tells me they must have occurred. Some things, which Mary told me of later, I do not remember at all. I can recall quite clearly the onset of my illness, and the feeling of relief and peace which accompanied it, although as it progressed it was not very peaceful. Such are the strange effects of shock upon the human physical and emotional make-up. And then of course, there is always the extra blow, the final card. But I am running ahead of my narrative.

I do not recall arriving at Victoria, or Mary meeting me there; but I do remember arriving at our house in Paddington, and feeling utterly confused; I had thought for some reason that we were going to Baker Street.

I remember reading the Reuther's despatch in the newspapers, much later it seemed to me — weeks, months later. 'But look,' I said to Mary, 'they say it only happened three days ago! How could it have taken so long for the news to reach England?' I remember that Mary was very kind.

The trial of the Moriarty gang was a long one, and the papers were full of it. All the evidence, of course, had been accumulated by Holmes, and his name was on everybody's lips. From time to time I found myself wondering who he was, this dead genius of whom the columnists wrote, this master detective whose career had ended so tragically at the age of thirty-seven. I was convinced that it was someone else of whom they spoke; someone whom I had never known, never loved. Apparently, I expressed my intention of attending every session of the trials, but Mary forbade it, and I only attended one or two. People recognised me, I think, as I sat in the public gallery. There were whispers, and several strangers greeted me respectfully. I regarded them warily. I was aware that for some reason I expected my name to be mentioned. I prepared myself to be summoned to the witness box; but I was not. I was surprised that the trial apparently had nothing to do with me. It seemed to have little to do with Professor Moriarty either, for his name was scarcely mentioned. This confirmed my opinion that the whole procedure was concerned with a different set of people entirely, and that the Mr Sherlock Holmes mentioned in connection with it was not my Holmes at all.

A large number of people were convicted, I remember. I did not recognise all the names; and one or two names I could have sworn having heard Holmes mention as ringleaders were not even brought forward.

Some time during the course of the trial, I think — though my memory has separated the two events entirely and I could have sworn that they happened in different years even — Mycroft Holmes arranged to meet me at Baker Street.

I had not been near the place since my return to London; and only once before (discounting the fact that he had been involved, in disguise, in transporting me from my house to Victoria Station on the morning of our departure from England) had I met Mycroft Holmes. I have placed that meeting on record in my account of the affair of 'The Greek Interpreter'. I remember how amazed I was at the time, that although the brothers lived in the same city, within walking distance of one another, they hardly ever saw each other. Recalling how close I had been to my own poor brother, I was perplexed. But when I saw them together in the bizarre environment of the Diogenes Club which was Mycroft's constant haunt,

I was less puzzled by their lack of intimacy. Eccentrics, both of them, they had grown to eye one another with suspicion, almost with distaste. Their goals, their priorities in life, were almost antithetical; and yet they shared the same intellectual powers, the same abilities of minute observation and lightning deduction. It had amused me, then, to see them together, and to observe the physical similarities and differences between them: Mycroft, the civil servant, obese and complacent; Sherlock, the consulting detective, thin, eager and unsatisfied.

A telegram and two letters had passed between myself and Mycroft Holmes in the wake of our mutual bereavement; my telegram to him from Meiringen; his letter to me which awaited me upon my return to London, in which he confirmed that his brother had indeed kept him informed of the events leading up to his departure from England, and had left the deposition of all his property, such as it was, in his hands. He expressed brief condolences, and exhorted us to comfort ourselves with the knowledge that 'Sherlock had died in the service of his country, and for the good of our society.'

I responded with a brief acknowledgement and condolences. I loathed the man. The knowledge that he, and not I, would have access to Baker Street and to all the treasured belongings which still no doubt lay scattered around what was once our shared lodgings, was almost insupportable. I could only suppose that Holmes had meant to be kind, in leaving the responsibility to him rather than to me; or maybe he had thought it best, considering that I also could have been in danger; or maybe he had merely opted to make the more conventional deposition to a relative, instead of to one who was merely a friend.

I remember that I spent a considerable time reading Mycroft's telegram, as though trying to decipher some underlying message in it.

'What is it, John?' asked Mary anxiously from across the breakfast table, and I handed it to her silently. It sounded simple enough when she read it aloud:

'Would be obliged if you could meet me at 3.00 this afternoon at S's old lodgings in Baker Street. Have instructions which I wish to discuss with you. Mycroft Holmes.'

'Would you like me to go with you?' offered Mary, but I declined, and wired to Mycroft that I would be there as arranged. Mary saw me off with some anxiety; she knew that I would find Baker Street and Mrs Hudson hard to bear, and was angry that Mycroft had not had the sensitivity to suggest meeting somewhere else.

It was the same, exactly the same. The yellow facade of Baker Street was warm and bright in the sun. My foot fitted comfortably into the slight depression in the second step; the clang of the bell when I rang was so familiar that I hardly noticed it.

'Oh, Dr Watson!' Mrs Hudson was overcome with emotion. I realised that it was my part to be strong and comforting, and I played it perfectly well. The smell of baking wafted up the stairs from the basement, and the afternoon sunlight fell across the landing just as it always had.

'Mr Holmes is upstairs,' sniffed Mrs Hudson, and I nodded vaguely and was about to proceed upwards when she corrected herself hastily — 'Mr Mycroft Holmes.'

The surprise on my face was delayed, and it must have appeared that the correction rather than the original statement caused the shock. I stumbled up the stairs on shaking legs.

It was the same, exactly the same. There were papers and books heaped in drifts in every corner. The chemical apparatus stood propped upon the coal scuttle. The mantelpiece was a mass of pens, cigarette ends, pipettes, syringes, small wooden boxes and screwed-up pieces of paper. The unpaid bills still hung impaled from the jack-knife at the centre. The Stradivarius lay in its case, propped up in my old armcahir; and Mycroft Holmes sat smoking in the other.

He rose as I entered, and perceiving I made no move towards him but stood dazedly letting my gaze wander round the room, approached me and held out his hand.

'So good of you to come, Dr Watson,' he said. 'Pray sit down.'

I took his hand mechanically. It reminded me, as I have remarked elsewhere, of the broad, fat flipper of a seal. I took in his massive, ungainly form, the square neck and fleshy jowls, the surprisingly firm small mouth. I met his eyes, and quickly looked away. They were a lighter, more watery grey than his, but the resemblance was unmistakeable. They had that introspective look which his had adopted when deep in concentration. And the line of the brows, the temples, was exactly the same.

Mycroft waved me to my chair, and removed the Stradivarius, which he lay carelessly upon the couch.

'That must be worth quite a lot,' he said, seeing my gaze fixed upon it. I said nothing. He reseated himself and offered me a cigarette. I accepted it and attempted to steady myself as I sucked in the smoke. I cleared my throat.

'You have not yet — been able to clear the room,' I said.

Mycroft grunted. 'Hmm, yes, this is why I sent for you. I thought it in order to let you know what my brother's instructions were concerning his property. You will probably find them . . . unconventional, but then, he was an unconventional man. As you know, Doctor.' He looked at me with what appeared to be a hint of suspicion. I merely nodded bleakly.

'You have been unwell, Dr Watson?' he asked smoothly, changing the subject with no explanation.

'Why — no,' I said, 'not really; that is, not more than' — than was to be expected, I had been going to say, but suddenly realised that I had better not.

'You look strained and tired,' continued Mycroft dispassionately. 'You have been following the trial?'

'Yes.'

'And how do you think it is going?' He eyed me keenly.

'Well, I — it seems to be going as expected. Your brother's evidence — is sure to convict?' The questioning note in my voice betrayed that my grasp of the trial's progress was in reality most feeble. Mycroft seemed satisfied, for he nodded twice and grunted.

'I hear that you have taken up your practice again,' was his next comment.

'Yes, on and off.' This was true. Mary had encouraged it and I seemed to be quite efficient.

'Excellent.'

I looked at him in surprise. He held his hands together, in almost the same way; but his fingers were neither long nor delicate enough. I frowned as I stared at them.

'So you will, I take it, be concentrating at last upon your medical career.'

My surprise increased. My career was nothing to me. I did not understand what he meant.

'You have refused an offer from *The Strand* magazine,' he said patiently.

How did he know that? Dimly it came back to me. They had indeed approached me for my account of the tragedy. Mary had been quite angry with them.

'I . . . yes, they did ask me to write something,' I said. 'But really, it is too soon — I could not.'

'Well, you were quite right of course. Especially as the trial is still in progress. They will probably approach you again; I don't think there would be any harm in it. The public will want to know.'

Was he saying that he *wanted* me to write an account of his brother's death?

'I . . . I really don't know that I can,' I said.

'Well, give it time. There would be no harm, as I said. But I think perhaps that should be all, don't you? No point in dragging up any other cases. I know you have taken copious notes . . .'

So that was it. How could he — how *could* he imagine that I planned to build up a literary career on my friend's memory? I felt my face contort with anger.

'I have no intention of publishing any further cases,' I said tightly. Mycroft grunted and stubbed out his cigarette in our ashtray. With an angry gesture, I did the same.

'What was it you wanted to discuss with me, Mr — Mycroft Holmes?' I said as calmly as I could. 'Or did you just invite me here to ensure that I keep my memoirs to myself?'

He was bland, smooth, unmoved. He rose massively from the chair. His small mouth was compressed, and he trod heavily across to the window, his hands clasped behind his back. I watched his huge form outlined against the familiar sunlight, and realised that I had read no grief in his eyes. His brother's death seemed hardly to have touched him, save to present him with the problem of disposing of his effects. And no wonder. He had hardly known him. He had never known him.

A sudden prickling of tears caused me to blink rapidly as I looked round once more at all the old, familiar objects. I could see Holmes' neat handwriting on the top of a sheaf of paper which lay in a heap next to the chair in which Mycroft had been sitting. Suddenly I could not bear that he should so much as handle, let alone dispose of, my beloved friend's belongings. And I, was I not to be allowed even to touch them?

Swiftly I rose and picked up the Stradivarius. I returned with it to my chair and opened the case. There it lay, the smooth, polished wood, the ebony chin-rest where his cheek had rested, the slim bow, its horsehair slack, which his long, sensitive fingers had held. The groove of the bow was clearly marked in the resin which I unwrapped from its soft cloth. He had made that groove in the amber. I closed the lid hastily. I felt Mycroft's eyes upon me.

'My brother's instructions,' he said, as though he had never intended to digress from the subject, 'are that his rooms be left untouched. Exactly as they are. His belongings are not to be moved. I have arranged it all with Mrs Hudson. She will receive more than the usual rent, so she has no cause for complaint.'

He watched my face. My amazement appeared to satisfy him.

The hint of a smile played about his lips.

'We agreed that Sherlock was an unconventional man,' he said.

My mind was racing. What on earth was he saying? For what, for whom were the rooms to be kept? What possible purpose could it serve? Why, why had Holmes never spoken to me about this?

'I don't understand.'

'There is very little to understand, Dr Watson. It is no great mystery. Sherlock wanted me to see to it that his rooms were kept just as they are.'

'But why, in heaven's name?'

Mycroft shrugged. 'Just one of his whims, I suppose. Would you say that he was a whimsical man, Dr Watson?'

I was silent for a while.

'This is senseless,' I said at last.

'Maybe. But it was his wish. I thought you ought to know. In case you found out from some other quarter and thought that I had neglected my duties as executor.'

I clutched at the violin case in my lap.

'You may take that, if you wish,' said Mycroft. 'He said you were to have anything you wanted.'

I looked at him.

'He said that he left the choice up to you. That you should be allowed to take anything you wanted to keep.'

My gaze travelled about the room again. This time I noticed that although dust lay upon the papers, the surfaces, it was only a thin layer, a few day's accumulation; that the spirit flask on the sideboard was half full.

'The bills will be paid,' said Mycroft, as my eyes rested upon the jack-knife.

It was bizarre, incredible. I could not believe that no purpose lay behind it.

'May I see the papers where he set down these instructions?'

'I'm afraid not, Dr Watson.' Mycroft padded across from the window and came to sit opposite me again. He leaned forward, his elbows on his knees.

'Why not?' I asked.

'Because they are confidential; they are addressed only to me, as his next of kin.'

I met his gaze. Bitterness and impotence overwhelmed me. His next of kin. But you neither knew him nor cared for him. You never loved him as I did. The words died unspoken on my lips. I tasted their blood.

The calm, watery gaze rested on me.

'I am well aware,' said Mycroft softly, 'that you were his intimate friend. But that does not give you the right to see his will, I'm afraid. As his brother, it is my duty to see that his instructions are carried out to the letter. I understand that you find them surprising; but really, you have no choice but to take them at face value.'

'But there must be some purpose behind them. I knew him better than you did. He never would have made such a stipulation out of mere sentimentality.'

My voice rasped in my throat. An unpleasant expression stole into the pale grey eyes.

'I would be very careful, Dr Watson, if I were you,' said Mycroft in soft, hissing tones, 'about making too much of your intimacy with Sherlock. Your habits are not unknown to me, nor are the circumstances of your accompanying my brother over to the Continent. Remember that he would not have had to place himself in danger were it not for you. I would not like to have to accuse you of adding slander to the other ills you brought upon him.'

The sun darkened at the window. The silence between us expanded and filled the room.

Mycroft rose and held out his plump white hand to me.

'So good of you to come, Dr Watson. I thought it would be best to tell you of the arrangements, and I would be delighted for you to keep the violin.'

Slowly, trembling, I rose and took his fingers briefly. My own were as cold as ice. I murmured something — I cannot remember what — and left the room, cradling the Stradivarius in my arms as though it were a child.

Haltingly I descended the stairs. I found Mrs Hudson at the bottom.

'Did Mr Mycroft Holmes explain it to you, sir? About the will?'

'Yes,' I whispered.

'And what do you think, Dr Watson? Don't you think it strange?'

'Yes, very.'

'But then, Mr Holmes was always very strange. I can't say that I like the idea, Dr Watson, but — well, there's the will, and there's the money. The money can't last forever, I suppose. Do you think' — her voice sank to a whisper and she looked furtively upwards — 'do you think Mr Mycroft Holmes has some kind of plans for those rooms, sir? I mean, what good is it to anyone, if they just stand empty?'

I shook my head. 'I don't know, Mrs Hudson. It's all very

strange. But it's really none of my business, you see; Mycroft Holmes is the next of kin . . .'

She opened the door for me and I stepped out into the sunlight. She bade me an affectionate farewell, saying that I was welcome to call in to the rooms whenever I wanted to.

'. . . It's as if he was planning to come back, isn't it Dr Watson?'

I whistled for a hansom.

On the journey home, I reflected that this sort of thing happened to so many of us. It was just that I had never thought that it would happen to me. Foolish, under the circumstances. I would have to warn Mary.

I also reflected that the thing Mycroft had said was true; he would never have left England at all, if it had not been for me.

For three days afterwards, I amazed both Mary and myself by my calmness and steadiness. I went about my work meticulously. I wondered if I had at last become anaesthetised, beyond caring. On the fourth day, I fell ill. Brain fever was diagnosed. I did not set foot outside the door for months.

## — *VII* —

AS I SAID earlier, I greeted the onset of my illness with relief. I experienced a delicious sense of letting go, setting adrift. My responsibilities were lifted from me; I could set down the burden of myself at the feet of others. It was up to them to carry me.

Mary told me afterwards that she too was relieved; my brave facade had worried her. She coped with my illness admirably. Many of her friends came to help and support her; Isobel Forrester, of course, and Anne D'Arcy, who once came and held my hand, I remember it vaguely. In what must have been periods of lucidity, I was aware that the house seemed full of women. I treated the awareness as another hallucination. Women, I thought, always hovered like ravens wherever there was sickness and death. How Holmes would have hated it! The idea struck me as hilariously funny. I remember lying back upon a heap of pillows, weak with laughter. Finding that their ministrations served only to exacerbate my condition, they at last had the good sense to leave me alone, so that I slept.

The main subject of my delirium appeared to be the confusion of

Mycroft Holmes with Moriarty. Apparently I told anyone who would listen that Mycroft was the Napoleon of Crime, that he had hounded his brother to death, and then been acquitted at the trial. Moriarty came to visit me in the guise of a respectable physician; he sat at my bedside, shaking his head slowly from side to side as Holmes had described. 'What have you done with him?' I shouted. 'How did you escape?' After he had gone, I tried to warn them not to be fooled by his respectable appearance. He might be a pillar of society, I said, but he was responsible for half that is evil and all that is undetected in the City of London. Who, they asked, who did I think I was talking about? Mycroft Holmes, I replied, Mycroft Holmes.

I called on Holmes constantly, of course. It was as well that only Mary and her friends heard me.

I recovered and was taken to Hastings, to Mrs Forrester's home to convalesce. It was May again. I sat by the sea on mild days. I interested myself in the bustle and chaos of the fish market. Sometimes I took a slow walk up the hill from the town and sat in the shadow of the old castle. It was beautiful, and almost against my will I regained my strength. One weekend, I remember, young Valentine came home for a visit. I was strangely moved by his youth and freshness. He played the violin to me. I showed him Holmes' Stradivarius, which I always kept with me. He took it from its case and held it reverently, wide-eyed; he did not attempt to play it, and I was pleased with his sensitivity. He awakened something in me; not exactly an enthusiasm for life and beauty, but an acceptance of it. By the time we returned to London, I was ready to take up my practice again.

Another year passed slowly and relatively uneventfully. *The Strand* approached me again, as Mycroft had predicted, through my literary agent Dr Conan Doyle. This time I agreed to write an account of my friend's last case. 'The Adventure of the Final Problem' I called it, knowing that no one would guess, from the heavily edited version which was published, the true nature of the problem to which it referred.

Moriarty's brother, a Colonel James Moriarty, had been writing letters to the press, defending his brother's memory which, he said, had been maligned and slandered at the trial. He accused Holmes of victimisation, and said that he had deliberately lured his brother to his death, knowing that he could not be convicted by an English court. There was much public interest in the matter, hence *The Strand's* invitation to me. I think I succeeded in setting matters straight; after my account was published, there were no more letters from Colonel James Moriarty.

It was my meeting with Dr Conan Doyle to discuss my response to *The Strand's* invitation which brought mme back for the first time to one of my old haunts, the Domino Room at the Cafe Royal. As I entered once more through the green swing doors, and walked with my own reflection past the long, gilded mirrors and blue pillars wreathed in vine leaves, I experienced a feeling of displacement, of alienation, for which I had not been prepared. The air was heavy with the smoke of cigars and Turkish cigarettes, and the patrons who lounged at the marble-topped tables were carefree and vain as they had always been; but I could no longer even pretend to number myself among them.

Dr Conan Doyle was sensible and kind; he asked me frankly whether I felt able to publish such an account as *The Strand* was asking for. I told him that under the circumstances I thought it important that I wrote something, and showed him the draft that I had already prepared. He said that he would read it through and let me have his comments. He looked at me keenly. I knew he was worried lest I had written anything indiscreet. He was a most meticulous editor. He was perceptive enough to be quite well aware of my feelings for Holmes, although he never referred overtly to the matter. His attitude, I knew, was one of pity, which I would have repudiated had he ever voiced it. He took the medical rather than the judgmental line.

I sipped at the excellent Beaune that he had ordered for us, and let my gaze wander around the room. I had never come here with Holmes; he eschewed the place — probably, I saw now, because he knew I visited it in other company. Now I stared blankly, unmoved, at my fellow guests, some of whom I recognised; and my sense of alienation increased. They were happy, carefree, all of them. In spite of the scandal that had accompanied the closure of Cleveland Street, there was a mood of optimism and carelessness among those who shared my persuasion, which seemed much more pronounced than it had been two years before. Some of the younger men wore green carnations; that fashion was obviously catching on. They were graceful and languid as young trees enjoying their first summer, unafraid, laughing on their journey into winter. I felt so old, so damaged.

Two young men in particular caught my attention. They must have been in their early twenties, both of them, one fair, one dark, both beautiful. They were talking animatedly over champagne and cigarettes. The golden-haired one held his head slightly to one side and toyed with the stem of his glass; his dark friend spoke emphatically, leaning forward, his keen eager features reflected in the mirror behind him.

About fifteen years ago, I thought, if we had known each other then; if I had been wealthy, and he unhurt — could we, would we have been like that?

They broke into delighted laughter; they sipped their champagne, their eyes engaged; the dark boy reached out and lightly touched the other's hand. I could bear it no longer. I finished my wine, and raised an eyebrow to Conan Doyle, indicating that it was time to leave. He, poor fellow, was more than pleased to do so; the Domino Room was not his milieu. At another time it would have amused me.

As we passed out through the doors, we encountered yet another golden lad, in a beautifully tailored light suit, with large, loosely-knotted tie and straw boater, carrying a gold-headed cane. He could not have been much over twenty-one, yet he carried himself with the assured and patronising air which bespeaks a privileged background. I turned back to look at him; he returned my gaze coolly, and looked away.

'Lord Alfred Douglas, I believe,' murmured Conan Doyle in my ear.

So that was he; I had heard the name. So much had happened in the last two years.

I should have warned them, I thought, as my hansom bore me swiftly back to Paddington; I should have warned them that they will not be allowed to be happy for long; that they will all suffer one day, as I have suffered; even the young ones, even the beautiful, even the rich. The Mycroft Holmeses of this world will make sure of that.

Apart from that one brief visit to the Domino Room, I made no attempt to resume my former haunts or my further companions. Only a handful of friends had bothered to enquire after me when I was ill; and at the age of forty, I crept thankfully into retirement, feeling too old and too exhausted to weather the storms that raged in the young. Also, I felt that I owed it to Holmes to live quietly; like a devoted widower, I pledged myself to celibacy.

Twice I walked along Baker Street and looked up at our old windows, picturing to myself the scene within, the empty, abandoned, grieving rooms. I could not bring myself to go in.

So absorbed was I in my own retirement, that I did not at first observe that Mary was looking ill. When at last it dawned on me, I was filled with alarm and anger.

'Why didn't you tell me that you were feeling unwell?' I asked, taking in for the first time the strained, transparent look to her face, the shadows and lines around her eyes, her thinness. She shrugged and gave an unconvincing laugh.

'It's not as bad as that, John. Just a few pains in the chest. Dr Anstruther says that rest is the best cure, and so I am resting. Haven't you noticed that I have become even lazier than usual?'

She leaned back languidly in her armchair, a bored expression on her face, trying to impersonate the manners of the idle rich. I gripped at the arm of my chair.

'Anstruther? You've been to see Anstruther behind my back? For heaven's sake, Mary, why didn't you come to me?'

My voice rose up the scale in alarm. Mary surveyed me through lowered lashes.

'My dear husband, it didn't seem quite decent. Rather incestuous, don't you think?'

'Of course not, what rubbish!' I snapped. She opened her eyes and smiled apologetically.

'Sorry, John. The truth was, I didn't want to bother you because you're still far from well yourself. How would you like to prescribe me a period of convalescence in Hastings? You could come down yourself, if you like.'

The thought of another spring in Hastings appealed to me, but something warned me that I should let her visit Mrs Forrester alone.

'You go,' I said. 'Go and rest. For God's sake, Mary,' I added peevishly, 'don't you dare die and leave me. If you do, I'll never forgive you!'

'What an extremely uncharitable attitude. I hope you don't say that to all your patients.' She patted my head as she glided out of the room.

When she died, a few weeks after her return from Hastings, I signed over all my rights to her effects and her money to Isobel Forrester. I did not care what the solicitors thought. It was the least, the very least I could do.

## — VIII —

MARY DIED AT the end of June, and for three months I continued to take care of my house and my practice. At this time some of my friends did, after all, remember me, and came to visit me, offering sympathy and company, neither of which I wanted. Then one day I received another telegram from Mycroft Holmes:

'Have message for you. Will call upon you at five-thirty if convenient. Mycroft Holmes.'

My first thought was that I should send a wire by return stating in no uncertain terms that I forbade him to set foot over my threshold. It was over two years since our last meeting, and I could still remember every word, every look. His impudence in announcing his intention to call on me in such a way filled me with rage. And yet I could not help but be curious. What message could he possibly have for me, and from whom? There was only one thing that we had in common; and I could not deny myself the chance of knowing anything that might bear reference to the memory of my beloved.

In the end, I sent neither a positive nor a negative reply; I merely waited to see whether he would turn up at the appointed hour.

He did. As the girl announced him and he walked into my study, I felt my heart constrict in spite of myself; the dark hair, the keen grey eyes.

He looked exactly the same. I rose, and briefly touched the heavy flipper he extended to me. I motioned him to the armchair and resumed my seat.

'You have altered since I saw you last, Dr Watson,' he said impassively. I inclined my head slightly but said nothing. I knew that I had changed; there were streaks of white in my hair around the temples, I was thinner, my face was lined.

'I was sorry to hear of your wife's passing,' he said. His gaze took in my mourning. I had not worn mourning for Holmes. It would not have been expected.

He sat back in the chair, fingertips together, nodding resignedly at my silence. He pursed his mouth, and his eyes appeared to linger on my watch chain.

'You said you had a message for me,' I said shortly, when I could bear it no longer. Mycroft sighed deeply, and reached into the inner pocket of his frock-coat.

'That is so.' He extracted a small packet and toyed with it, passing it from hand to hand. 'I must warn you in advance, Dr Watson, that I can answer no questions concerning this article or how it passed into my hands. It is only under repeated pressure that I hand it over to you. I have resisted all such pressures in the past, and still believe that I was right to do so. But now, it seems, I have no choice. If you wish to follow it up, you are quite at liberty to do so. If you choose to ignore it, there will be no repercussions. I am passing it over to you as instructed, and I take no further responsibility.'

I leaned back in my chair, and glanced several times from his face to the small brown packet in his fingers. Something in his voice, something in his very reluctance to place the packet in my hands, set every nerve a-tingle. I was sure now that the message had something to do with Holmes. Some instructions he had left, something to do with me, which his brother out of viciousness or greed had hitherto ignored. I held out my hand, palm upwards. Mycroft sighed again, and placed the packet in my palm.

Its weight suggested to me that it was some article of jewellery. It was tied and knotted with thin, waxed string. I picked at the knot, then reached for my paper-knife. Resting the packet on the table, I sawed through the string and opened the layers of creased, brown paper. I saw the gleam of a chain.

I smoothed out the wrapping paper deliberately, and looked at the watch that lay face downward upon a piece of folded notepaper. My hand was shaking now, as I picked it up and gently turned it over so that it rested face upwards in my hand. It was neat and plain, as was always his taste in jewellery. The case was unmarked. The small, neat Roman numerals, the delicate hands, stared up at me from the white face, so utterly familiar. The chain was slim, the clasp unobtrusive; but there, yes, hanging from the chain, neatly pierced, was the gold sovereign which Irene Adler had given him when he, disguised as a groom, had acted as witness to her marriage. He had laughed about it at the time, saying that he would have it pierced for his watch-chain as a keepsake. It had surprised me that he, with his usual dislike of ornaments, had actually done so. It had become rather a joke between us.

I held the watch and gazed at it until I felt the tears start in my eyes.

'Where did you get this?' I whispered.

Mycroft Holmes, watching me keenly, did not reply.

I lifted it to my ear and heard the light, regular tick. It was working, then. But how had it survived — he had been wearing it when we left Meiringen. I knew that he had been wearing it. He had taken it out to check the time just before I turned back down that fateful path, to check that I would be able to join him for dinner at Rosenlaui. I could see him standing with the Falls behind him, looking at his watch, looking up at me, his grey eyes bleak and anxious; suddenly smiling as he put his watch away, smiling and clasping my hand, trying to reassure himself.

'In Rosenlaui, then.'

But he had never reached Rosenlaui. And the watch had plunged with him into the foaming cauldron of the waters.

I laid it back on the table. I looked at the silent Mycroft. His eyes revealed nothing; not the merest flicker.

Slowly, hesitantly, I reached for the folded square of thin white notepaper which still lay at the centre of the wrapping. I fumbled with it, aware that my shaking hands, the tear which glided slowly down my cheek, betrayed me utterly.

There was no message; only an address: 'Hôtel des Deux Mondes, Paris.' The handwriting was his.

It seemed an age before I could speak, or move, or think. The shock dried my tears, and I sat frozen in my chair, holding the note in my numb fingers. Mycroft said nothing.

At length I looked up at him. He was watching me distantly, curiously, as though observing the behaviour of some exotic animal.

'Where did you get this?' I demanded again. My voice had shrivelled to a croak.

'I told you in advance, Doctor, that I cannot answer that question. My instructions were simply to give you the package. That I have done. And now, if you please, I must bid you good day.'

He rose as he spoke, and took his hat from the table. He made no further attempt to shake hands.

'But instructions from whom?' I pleaded. Mycroft shook his head.

'Good day, Dr Watson,' he said, and left the room, closing the door behind him. I heard his heavy tread descending the stair. I ran to the door, opened it, and looked over the bannister; I watched him as he let himself out of the front door.

I turned back into the room, to the note and the watch upon the table. I poured over them for an hour or so, studying them, holding them, raising them to my lips, my cheek. At last I made an effort to pull myself together, pouring myself a generous measure of brandy and lighting a cigarette.

Who had sent Mycroft Holmes the watch? Who had instructed

him — had pressed him, he had admitted that he had brought it to me under pressure — to deliver it into my hands with this note? The obvious answer was impossible; it could not be, it was someone else, someone who wished to communicate with me. But how — ? They must have found the body, then. After all this time. Why had I not been told?

Mycroft. They had told Mycroft, and he had withheld the information from me. But the note? It was recent, it was dry; it was written in soluble ink. I studied it again, every curve, every stroke. It was, it was his hand. It was impossible that anyone else had written it. It was impossible that it had been found, after all that time, in his clothing. It could have been found at Baker Street, of course; but by whom? And the watch . . ?

A second brandy cleared my head. I sat down quietly as dusk crept into the room.

'When you have eliminated the impossible, whatever remains, however improbable, must be the truth.'

It was his favourite maxim.

But my mind could scarcely credit it.

## — *IX* —

I LEFT FOR Paris the following morning, on the same Continental express which Holmes and I had taken two and a half years ago from Victoria Station.

My journey was smooth and relatively swift, although in my agony of impatience every minute seemed unbearably long. I had no idea of who awaited me at the Hôtel des Deux Mondes, or how long my stay would be. I had packed and arranged for a fortnight; that seemed a reasonable length of time. Mycroft would no doubt hear of my departure without surprise; would he send news of my expected arrival to Paris? I did not know.

My trepidation, my confusion, may well be imagined. Again and again, I told myself that there was no way that he could have possibly survived that plunge into the roaring waters; that it could not possibly be he who awaited me. Better to think that it was some message, some clue, some mutual friend.

And there was another reason for pushing the thought from my mind. He could not — it was unthinkable that he would still be alive and not have contacted me. That he had left me all this time to think him dead; that he had sent me no word, no message, when he knew what I must be suffering.

I gazed blankly out of the window at the rolling Kentish countryside; at the receding white cliffs and the pitching green waters of the Channel; at the wide, flat fields of the French landscape, some green, some brown, denuded, their harvests gathered. Tall poplars leaned darkly against a pale sky, fruit trees glittered in the late sun. It was late in the evening when I arrived at the Gare du Nord. A small, ragged boy, seeing my air of hesitation and sensing no doubt that my knowledge of French and of French currency was likely to be minimal, took charge of my portmanteau in a most capable manner and led me through the throng to the cab stand.

'Pour où, m'sieur?' he demanded roughly.

I realised that I had only the name of the hotel, and neither the street nor the district. I showed my precious notepaper with Holmes' writing upon it, and stammered out the name in my imperfect French. 'Hôtel des Deux Mondes,' he repeated to the driver, who nodded, to my relief, in a perfectly sanguine manner.

'Deux Mondes, bon, m'sieur. Montez!'

'Merci, m'sieur!' shrilled the urchin, having hoisted my portmanteau onto the rack, and held out his hand with an endearing lack of subtlety. I pressed some coins into it, and he seemed satisfied. I climbed into the cab and we rattled off.

I had never travelled in foreign parts alone before, I realised. It was quite amusing. My time in the Army had made me a seasoned traveller, but it came to me as something of a shock that neither then nor in my subsequent travels with Holmes had I really had to take care of myself in a foreign land. My French being only just passable, I began to wonder how well I would succeed in making myself understood, should I find no one waiting for me at the hotel. Holmes of course had spoken perfect French, the result of long holidays with his French grandmother during his boyhood and early youth.

I glanced out at the gas-lit streets and unfamiliar shop-fronts, the furled awnings and dark windows. Here and there the light streamed out from a restaurant or club, and I heard loud, harsh voices and bursts of laughter. There were leaves on the pavement, under the gas lamps. In a surprisingly short time we had reached the hotel. Light from its porch flooded the pavement, and a footman hurried out to take my portmanteau while I entered upon a painful negotiation with the driver about the fare. When all was finally completed, I followed the man into the red-carpeted vestibule, plushly furnished in gilt and velvet, and made my way to the desk, feeling conspicuous in the glare of the lights, and mentally rehearsing my enquiry.

The first exchange was straightforward enough; no, there was no Englishman by the name of Mr Sherlock Holmes staying at the hotel; nor had there been; nor was he expected.

So that was that. My heart sunk slowly to my boots.

But who was enquiring? Did I wish a room for the night? My friend would perhaps be arriving tomorrow?

I gave my name and said that yes, I would like to take a room. I was exhausted. The desk clerk turned to the ledger before him and gave an exclamation of surprise. My name again? Dr John Watson, from London? But yes, I was expected. A room had already been reserved for me, since yesterday. But my friend, Monsieur Sigerson, was expecting me — did I not know?

I must have looked extremely stupid. The man repeated the information in broken English. 'Monsieur Sigerson. 'E place a room for you. I 'ave 'ere ze key.'

'Sigerson?' I repeated blankly.

'Mais oui, monsieur. Vous ne le connaissez pas? Monsieur Sigerson. From Norvège,' he added.

From Norway? But I knew no Norwegians. It was true that Holmes had once worked on a case for the King of Scandinavia, but he had never mentioned the name Sigerson. The connection of Holmes with Norway in my mind, slight though it was, prompted me to make no further difficulties in my present situation.

'Ah, Monsieur Sigerson!' I said, as though the name had registered with me for the first time. 'Bon. Merci, monsieur.'

I accepted the key from the bemused clerk and allowed the page to lead me to my allotted room.

It was very comfortable, luxurious even; I immediately began to worry about the bill. But there was little I could do in the present circumstances. The reservation had been made for me; presumably all I had to do was wait. I enquired of the page which was Monsieur Sigerson's room. It was just two doors along the corridor from my own, he replied. Was he in? I asked calmly; no, he usually came in very late, sometimes not at all.

That sounds like him, I thought.

Dazedly I began to unpack, wandering now and then to the window to look out. It overlooked a spacious boulevard, lined with trees. The gas lamps shed pools of light onto the pavement. There was a small, wrought-iron balcony, probably intended for decoration rather than for the weight of a grown man; I decided that it would be unwise to try and stand upon it. A light supper was brought for me, but I could not eat much of it. I sat on the edge of the bed, holding my aching head in my hands and wondering when and how Mr Sigerson would reveal himself to me. Was he Holmes, under an alias? He used to have so many. But if it were he, the question remained — not only 'How?', but more importantly, 'Why, why, why?'

I paced the room, ate, unpacked, ran my fingers through my hair. I ordered a large brandy and drank it. When eventually I looked at my watch, I saw that it was three o'clock in the morning. There was nothing I could do but try and get a few hours' sleep.

I slept for about six hours and dreamed I was travelling through Norway on the Continental express. When I awoke, it took me some time to remember where I was and why; but as soon as I did so, I washed and dressed hurriedly and made my way downstairs. I lingered briefly at the door of his room; it was shut, locked. There was a different clerk on duty at the reception desk. I enquired whether Monsieur Sigerson had come in last night, and if so whether he had come down yet. Yes, the man replied, he had come in during the early hours of the morning; but he had risen early and had left the hotel about an hour ago. I sighed.

I gave the clerk my name and asked whether Monsieur Sigerson had enquired for me before he went out. Yes, came the reply, he had, and had been told of my arrival.

I decided that it would be sensible for me to have some breakfast, and made my escape in the direction of the *salle-à-manger*. I seated myself at a small table near the window and ordered a coffee and croissant. When it arrived, I sipped at the coffee but found that I was too shaken to eat.

He was here, and he knew that I was here. Why had he gone out? Was he avoiding me? Was he perhaps as nervous as I was?

I let my gaze wander blankly round the room and out of the window. There were pleasant gardens outside and a spacious avenue, lined with poplars. The autumn sunlight played among the dark leaves. I felt suddenly drawn to the outside, to the sunlight and air; I felt that I should go mad if I just went back to my room and waited. I rose hurriedly and made my escape, leaving my breakfast untouched upon the table.

I wandered out into the hotel grounds and soon found myself in the avenue, which was nearly deserted. I walked the length of it, slowly, calmly, half mesmerised by the flicker of light and shade as the sun moved above me behind the trees. Ahead of me I saw the boulevard, full of noise and colour and bustle. I toyed with the idea of walking on and losing myself in the city, wandering down to the river perhaps, taking in the sights, the atmosphere. But a surge of panic at the thought of wandering too far from the hotel caused me to turn back. As I retraced my steps, I saw a figure detach itself from one of the trees ahead of me, and begin slowly to advance towards me; a tall figure, dressed in black. I stopped in my tracks. I registered its approach, in top hat, frock-coat and gloves. Every line, every movement cried out to me.

He moved slowly through light and shade, light and shade, between the trees, along the path towards me. My heart beat wildly and I trembled in every limb, but I could not move. My tongue was dry in my mouth. Closer and closer he came, through bars of sunlight and shadow. At one stage he seemed to stay static, though still pacing, neither advancing nor retreating. I blinked away the illusion, and realised that he was very close now. I could almost see his face; then I could see it. White, a white face, with hooded eyes. I could see the firm line of his mouth. I could see the hollows under his cheekbones. He reached up, and removed his hat. I could see the line of his brow, his black hair, smooth in the sun. He had almost reached me; he stood before me.

I think I would have fallen if he had not caught me by the shoulders. I looked into the tired, white face, the clear grey eyes which glistened with tears. I noted the new lines around them and around his mouth; the sunken cheeks; the higher expanse of brow. I felt his grip upon my shoulders, and reached up to grip his in turn. Without knowing what I did, I drew him toward me and kissed him.

## — *X* —

HE DID NOT attempt to disengage me at once; and when he did, he took me gently by the arm and led me slowly back along the path. He looked round discreetly, I in alarm; but the avenue was nearly deserted. Looking behind I saw two people staring after us; but we walked slowly and calmly away from them.

I held tightly to his arm, for I was still weak and trembling, and could not walk fast. He sensed this and matched his pace to mine.

'Back to the hotel, my dear fellow,' he said quietly. 'You need a brandy.'

I turned to look at him; he had replaced his hat, and looked straight in front, his head held high. He turned to me briefly. The tears still shone in his eyes, and he looked away again as they met mine.

'Where did you go this morning?' I asked. I was surprised by the calmness of my voice.

'Nowhere. I followed you.'

'I didn't see you,' I said.

'That is what you should expect, when I follow you.' He smiled briefly. 'I thought it would be better to wait for you outside.'

'Yes.'

We walked on slowly in silence.

'I knew you would come,' he said.

'Yes.'

'Did you have a good crossing?'

'Yes, thank you.' I swallowed hard. It was strange; there was so much to say, that I could think of nothing.

'You are — using the name of Sigerson,' I said at last.

'Yes.'

'Why?'

'Because I am in danger. But not for much longer, I hope. I will explain, at the hotel.'

I moistened my lips. Danger? He was still in danger?

'How long have you been in Paris?' I ventured.

'For nearly two months.'

'Oh.'

I could not trust myself to ask him anything further. We reached the hotel in silence. Holmes led me to the bar.

'Ah, vous vous êtes trouvés, messieurs!' said the desk clerk happily as we passed.

'Oui, et merci monsieur,' responded Holmes, as he guided me across the vestibule. I tried to smile.

We found a secluded table in a corner of the bar and Holmes ordered coffee and brandy. He reached into his coat for his cigarette case; I took out his old silver one, which he had left with the note at Reichenbach, and slid it across the table to him. He picked it up and stared at it numbly.

'Thank you.'

He looked up suddenly, into my face. His own was pinched and drawn with anxiety. 'I thought it would be — better to give you time to settle in,' he said. 'Was I right?'

'Yes,' I said gently, though I would not have relived the last twelve hours for anything in the world.

'You look thin and ill,' he said falteringly, his eyes still fixed upon my face.

'How did you expect me to look?'

His eyes pleaded with me.

'You don't look well yourself,' I added more kindly; and indeed there was a dead white tinge to his skin which told me that his life recently had not been a healthy one, and that his cocaine habit had as strong a hold over him as ever.

He waved his hand. 'It's nothing, nothing. It has been dangerous and difficult, that's all.'

Dangerous, again.

The waiter brought our drinks. I ignored my coffee and took the brandy gratefully, swallowing its fire. Now, I will ask him now, I thought, lighting my cigarette.

'What is the danger?'

He seemed relieved. 'Two of Moriarty's henchmen are on my trail. Ralph Spencer and Sebastian Moran.'

I vaguely remembered the names. 'They — weren't at the trial,' I said.

He shook his head, avoiding my eyes. 'No, they both had good connections. They both slipped the net. Spencer is here in Paris. He does not yet know who I am; but he is looking for me and suspects that I am here. I have been lying low; but now I hear that he is dying. A duel, he was wounded in a duel. It may be a mere rumour, of course, a ruse. But if it is true, I will soon be out of immediate danger. Colonel Moran, however, is in England. In London. That is why I cannot return there, yet. If I do, and he hears of it, he will not rest until he has achieved his purpose. He is the only one left. If I bide my time, I will catch him unawares, and put him where he can do no further harm. Then — then I can come back to life.'

Again he raised his eyes swiftly to mine. I swallowed the rest of my brandy.

'Moriarty . . .' I said.

'Is dead.'

'I just wondered.' Don't, I said to myself, but I could not help myself. He waited. 'Where were you before you were here in Paris?' I decided the only way to approach it was to work backwards.

'Montpellier. Before that, Persia. Lhassa, before that.'

I stared at him. 'That sounds — delightful.'

He swirled the brandy in his glass. His long, nervous fingers picked at the tablecloth. 'No,' he said, 'no, it was not delightful.'

There was a short silence. Then he said quietly, 'I would have contacted you, Watson, if I could. But it was too dangerous.'

'You contacted Mycroft.' There was no stopping me now.

'I . . . yes. Because of his government connections, you see. I could reach him through diplomatic channels. Because I needed money.'

'Yes, I see. I suppose that would be important.'

Another brandy. Another cigarette.

'What did he say to you?' His voice was flat, hopeless.

'About the rooms. Your wish, he said. That they be kept the same.'

'Only that?'

'And that he was next of kin, and that I had no right to see the will.'

There was a look in his eyes that I can only describe as fear.

'Did you go there? To Baker Street?'

'Not after my interview with him there.'

'But — then — what did he say?'

'He said I could keep the Stradivarius. I took it away with me.'

'Anything. I said, anything you wanted.'

'He said that the bills would be paid. He said that I could publish an account of your death, but no more cases. He said that my habits were not unknown to him, and that I should be careful of making too much of my intimacy with you, and that I must remember that you would never have put yourself in danger if it were not for me.'

Holmes looked utterly aghast. I was pleased.

'Oh . . . God. But I thought — he said that you — were all right.'

'All right?' I nearly choked.

'He said — he didn't tell me you were ill, and I found out. I tried to contact you. But he said that the risk was too great. That you were under surveillance because of your indiscretions. That they would destroy you, and trace me. Then I heard' — he nodded at my clothes — 'about Mary. But I — he . . .'

He trailed off. Mercilessly I stared him down. My lips were numb, but I forced them to speak.

'Did you think I was anything other than destroyed already? Did you think I had any will or desire left for indiscretions, when I thought you were dead? Did you think that I cared for my reputation, when one word — one note, one token, could have let me know, oh God, that you were still alive? How could you, how *could* you, when you knew — that I loved you?'

The tears started to my eyes in earnest now. I did not know how to keep myself from breaking down. Hastily I gulped more brandy and stared desperately into his haunted face.

'Tell me, did you work it all out beforehand? Was that what you sat up all night thinking about, that night in Meiringen? How to escape without anyone knowing? Was that when you wrote your farewell note? A brilliant piece of composition, by the way — I still have it, would you care to read it over? I expect you counted on the fact that my hysterics would be convincing. The only thing I don't understand is how you faked all those footprints, and none coming back. Quite a remarkable achievement, that, but obviously not beyond the scope of your genius. Oh God.'

The tears were running down my face. Quickly Holmes finished his brandy, and came round the table to me.

'Let's go to your room. Come, try to be calm until we get there. Let me help you; don't worry, they will see your mourning and think it's that. Here, lean on my arm.'

I did as he told me, hastily dabbing at my eyes and keeping my gaze fixed upon the red floor. I heard the waiter murmur an anxious enquiry as we passed, and Holmes' low reply, in which I caught the words, 'sa femme' and 'en chambre, s'il vous plait'. I heard other murmurs of sympathy. Then we were on our way up the stairs. I do not think I could have found my room again, but Holmes led me there. I fumbled in my pocket for the key and handed it to him. He let us in, and shut the door firmly behind us.

I sank down on the edge of the bed, my head in my hands. I felt Holmes come to sit beside me. He took my wrists and gently drew my hands away from my face. To my own surprise, I jerked them away from his grasp.

'No,' I said roughly, 'leave me. Tell me. Tell me from the beginning.'

Sitting quietly on the bed, with his hands clasped on his knees, and his gaze fixed upon the lower right-hand corner of the door, he told me what happened that day at Reichenbach.

Moriarty and Ralph Spencer had found him at the Falls. They both had guns; he was unarmed.

'They came from different directions, and I was trapped. They threatened me. They threatened you. They said it was not too late for me to withdraw my evidence at the trial; and if I did not, they would kill us both, and make sure that our joint reputation was held open to question back in England. Moriarty would kill me, the other would overtake you on your way back to Meiringen. I offered to bargain, if they would leave you unharmed. I said I would discuss the matter with Moriarty alone.'

He had managed to persuade Spencer to go back to the main path with the boy, who was, as had been suspected, in their pay. He had written the note with Moriarty's gun trained on him; no doubt the latter had calculated that a farewell note would be to his advantage, if he were unable to persuade Holmes to agree to his conditions, and were forced to kill him. But Holmes, unarmed though he was, managed to overpower and disarm his antagonist.

'We tottered together upon the brink of the Falls. I have some knowledge, however, of baritsu, or the Japanese system of wrestling, which has more than once been very useful to me. I slipped through his grip, and he with a horrible scream kicked madly for a few seconds, and clawed the air with both his hands. But for all his efforts he could not get his balance, and over he went. With my face over the brink, I saw him fall for a long way. Then he struck a rock, bounded off, and splashed into the water.'

Shaken and exhausted, Holmes' one thought had been to escape; not only from Spencer and whoever else might be on his trail, but also from himself, and from his association with me. Moriarty's threats had struck home at his most vulnerable point; his confusion and ambivalence, his jealousy and despair about our friendship. It had been the decision of a moment, a decision made in panic; he had climbed up the rock, which was not quite as sheer as it appeared. It was a terrifying and difficult climb.

'I seemed to hear Moriarty's voice screaming at me out of the abyss. A mistake would have been fatal. More than once, as tufts of grass came out in my hand or my foot slipped in the wet notches of the rock, I thought that I was gone. But I struggled upward, and at last I reached a ledge several feet deep and covered with soft green moss. I collapsed upon it and lost consciousness. I must have been out for a long time. It was night by the time I recovered. It was a moonlit night. I looked over the edge. There were footprints everywhere. My cigarette case was gone from the boulder. Someone had found the message.

'I could not go back to Meiringen; I had, to all appearances, killed an innocent man, and if I rejoined you, they would know me to be alive, and pursue us both. I could not go on to Rosenlaui; they would be waiting there, just in case. They must think me dead; let them go on thinking that, it was safest, until you got back to London and the trial was over. Somehow I ran ten miles over the mountains in the darkness, and a week later I found myself in Florence, with the certainty that no one in the world knew what had become of me.'

I stirred, and he paused.

'You did not hear me calling you?'

'No.'

Of course not. The waters.

'You were lying up there, unconscious, all the time?'

'Yes.'

I could not believe it. I thought that I would have known, if he were there. But the place had been empty; deserted. As if he had merged into the torrent of water.

'I came back,' I said. 'Twice.'

He was quiet. 'I did not know,' he said.

There was a silence; then he continued.

He had meant to communicate with me, he said. He had never intended that I should think him dead for long. But when he had contacted Mycroft, through diplomatic channels, and asked him to deliver some discreet message to me, Mycroft had warned of the scandal and danger and advised him to wait until after the trial.

The trial had gone badly, in that Spencer and Moran were not touched. Holmes, now hearing that I had been ill, had again asked his brother to contact me, and this time was told that I was under surveillance, and that the slightest indication on my part that I knew him to be alive would lead his enemies straight to him. Apparently Mycroft assured him that I had plenty of friends to comfort me, and would certainly be all right. He also spoke of my wife; her security, what she deserved.

'I should not have believed him' — Holmes looked up at me at last, and our eyes held — 'I know what he thought. But I chose to believe him. What can I say? I remembered that you judged things differently. And I was travelling, meeting new people, imbibing new ideas. It seemed to me that freedom was within my grasp. The possibility of a completely new life. And I thought that if I cut you out of my heart — '

He stopped abruptly, unable to continue. It was not in his nature to weep, but he closed his eyes while I wept for him.

When he could proceed, he told me of his work under the name of Sigerson. Mycroft had been pressing him to work for the Government, and he did for a while, in Khartoum. Then he came back to France and settled in Montpellier; a laboratory commissioned him to research into coal-tar derivatives.

Spencer and Moran meanwhile had found out that he was alive, and so the game of cat-and-mouse was resumed.

'I came to Paris, and Spencer followed me here. Moran, I knew, had gone back to London. I sent for news, through my contacts, and that was how I heard about your — about Mary. It was a great shock. I contacted Mycroft again, and forced his hand. I told him that as far as I was concerned, I now had nothing to lose; and if he did not give my token to you, I would return publicly to London to find you myself.'

The smooth, flat monotone of his voice cased. There was silence in the room. The sounds from the boulevard below drifted up and clustered against the window; they came from outside, from another world.

Then abruptly, I buried my face in my hands and sobbed uncontrollably. Once I had begun, I found that I could not stop.

I felt his hand on my shoulder.

'Watson,' he said. 'Don't.'

I could not stop. His hand moved lightly over my hair. And again.

'Please.'

I struggled with my breath. I heaved into silence, with only the occasional sob. Through every nerve in my body, I felt his hand upon my hair.

Suddenly, there was a knock at the door.

'Entrez,' said Holmes' voice from the other side of the room. I looked through my fingers, and saw a man enter with a small table, followed by others with plates and salvers, a bottle and glasses. Silently they laid the table with *pâté*, cold fowl, salad.

'I ordered lunch up here,' said Holmes from the window. 'I thought you would prefer it.'

When they had gone, I recovered myself while he poured the wine. We talked, and ate.

We talked all afternoon. We spoke of Mary; of Herr Steiler; of the trial, of Spencer and Moran. Holmes told me a little about Lhassa; but it was too painful for me to hear him speak of places and people he had encountered when I thought him dead, and I asked him to stop. We spoke instead of Baker Street, picking up the threads of the old days.

Later, we went for a walk. The cool evening breeze revived me somewhat, and I experienced a childlike wonder, gazing up at the lamplight in the trees as we passed beneath them. We dined at a garish little restaurant on the Boulevard St Michel. Holmes, as I looked at him across the chequered tablecloth, actually looked happy. There was a smile around his eyes as he met my gaze.

It was only when we were halfway through our meal that he asked me again about Mycroft — how he had delivered his message to me, what he had said. His lips set into a thin, hard line as he heard my account of it.

'I'm sorry,' he whispered, 'I'm sorry.'

His eyes searched my face.

'Watson,' he said, 'forgive me. Please.'

It was as though a rainbow were arching back over the wasteland of the last few years. My face must have shown what I felt.

'I forgive you, my dear Holmes,' I said softly.

'Thank you.' The smile returned to his face and he poured us both more wine.

I drank far too much that evening. Following the brandies and the wine at lunch, it was enough to render me almost incapable. The emotional strain of the last twenty-four hours and the previous night's lack of sleep no doubt did much to enhance the effect. When we arrived back at the hotel, Holmes helped me out of the cab and up the stairs to my room. Even in my drunken state, I relished every sign of tenderness and concern. He made me drink some water.

'My poor Watson, you're exhausted,' he said. 'Here, let me help you with your collar. Don't bother to undress, just sleep now, as you are. You'll feel all right in the morning.'

With the briefest of preparations, I made ready. Holmes pulled the quilt over me.

'Sleep now,' he said. 'I will be just along the corridor. I will see you in the morning.'

'Don't go,' I tried to say, raising myself on the pillow. 'Don't go. I am afraid of not seeing you again.' I remember that panic rose in my throat, and that he calmed me, taking my hand.

'I won't go,' he said. 'I will stay here until you are asleep. I promise.'

I slept fitfully, and woke perhaps an hour or so later, to find him lying beside me, exhausted. He had not gone back to his room, then; he had fallen asleep, sitting up with me.

'Holmes,' I murmured blearily, 'you'll get cold. Come under the covers.' I pulled the quilt over him.

'Thank you,' he said, though his eyes remained closed, and he moved closer to me. As unobtrusively as I could, I put my arms round him.

'Thank you,' he murmured again, and settled his head upon my shoulder.

I measured my breathing to his, and lay quietly, stroking the dark head on my shoulder, until I too fell asleep.

## — *XI* —

I AWOKE TO the smell of coffee. Holmes stood by the window, looking fresh and relaxed in his shirtsleeves, cup and saucer in hand, absorbed in the activity of the boulevard below.

As I stirred, he turned, and gave me a quick smile.

'Awake, Watson? Have some coffee. I took the liberty of ordering breakfast for you. It should be here in a minute.'

I sat up slowly, realising that I was still in my day clothes, and that my head felt sore and fragile.

'You'll feel better when you've breakfasted,' said Holmes, coming to pour some coffee from the pot which stood on the bedside table.

I accepted the cup and saucer from him and sipped at the hot beverage. My eyes searched his face anxiously. He seemed perfectly sanguine, as if nothing had happened. Nothing *had* happened, I reminded myself hastily, as the coffee cleared my thoughts. He was washed, shaved and dressed already. He must have slipped out of bed some time ago, leaving me to sleep on.

There was a knock at the door, and a waiter entered, bearing a tray with a salver upon it, which he placed before me on the bed. Holmes nodded politely at him, and he left. I lifted the salver, and an appetising smell of hot scrambled eggs filled the room. I realised that I was hungry.

'Aren't you having any?' I asked.

Holmes smiled. 'I breakfasted on fresh croissants,' he said, 'about an hour ago.'

'What time is it then?' I saw that the morning must be well advanced.

'Almost ten-thirty, my dear Doctor. You have slept well. And when you have breakfasted and made yourself look decent, I intend to introduce you to Paris by daylight. A stroll will do you the world of good.'

He was right. As we walked arm in arm along the banks of the Seine, lingering at the stalls of the *bouquinistes*, breathing in the autumn breeze which stirred the sunlight among the dark, thinning leaves of the trees, I felt an upsurge of strength and well-being such as I had not experienced for years. The wine from last night which still sang in my veins served only to lend a transparent, keen quality to our surroundings. I will never forget that morning, that walk. I could scarcely believe that twenty-four hours could have wrought such a change.

Occasionally Holmes would halt abruptly and peer after some figure in the crowd or after a passing carriage.

'Have you heard any news of Ralph Spencer?' I asked, as we sat in the shady doorway of a cafe, sipping at a beverage of *chocolat froid*, a delight that was new to me and which promised to become addictive.

'Not yet,' he answered. 'But I do have contacts here, and they will let me know immediately there is any news one way or the other.' He sighed. 'We can only hope that the rumours are true. If Spencer dies, only Moran will be left, and he cannot evade justice forever. It is only a matter of time.'

He turned to me with a hesitant, anxious look on his face.

'What arrangements did you make, Watson, before you left England? Can you stay here indefinitely?'

'I hardly had time to make any,' I said. 'I said that I might be away for a fortnight. Anstruther is minding my practice.'

He looked at me almost shyly, and passed a hand over his sleek black hair.

'Will you stay here with me indefinitely?' he asked. 'I cannot return yet; I have to wait until the coast is clear for me. It may be a few months, and I think — if you were with me, it would not seem so long.'

I was so moved by his faltering manner that I could only whisper my reply.

'I will stay.'

'Thank you,' he said.

That afternoon I sent a wire to Anstruther. It was all most irregular, I knew. Probably I would have no practice to go back to. Luckily, I had acquired a capable housekeeper after Mary's death; at least I need not worry that the household would sink into chaos. I was careful to make arrangements about the servants' wages.

'I suppose your brother will hear of all this,' I said to Holmes. 'What will he do?'

'There is nothing he can do.' Holmes' mouth had set into a thin, hard line. I felt a fierce stab of joy.

He turned back to the mirror to complete his preparations. We were going to dine out again, at his insistence. I sat on the bed and looked around at his room, at the accumulation of paraphernalia he had picked up on his travels.

A soapstone Buddha sat smooth and complacent upon the mantelpiece, glowing softly in the light from the gas bracket. A carved ivory shoe-horn lay beside it, its handle writhing with fantastic beasts and small, intricate flowers. A small but gorgeous Persian rug was draped over the back of the armchair. But the *pièce de résistance* sat on a high-backed chair by the window.

It was a wax bust of Holmes, a perfect, even an alarming likeness. He said that it had been modelled in Grenoble; he appeared to be inordinately proud of it. The expression was one of fierce repose, the profile was aquiline, noble. A smile of amusement came to my face as my eyes rested upon it, and I bit my lip.

'You are so vain, Holmes.'

He was knotting his dress tie, looking down his nose at his own reflection. He followed my gaze in the mirror.

'It's a very good likeness, Watson,' he said peevishly. 'True art is the mirror of nature.'

'Not according to the latest theories,' I said, 'which state quite convincingly that nature is but a poor imitation of art.' I favoured him with a swift, unpleasant smile as he turned to me from the mirror.

'Monsieur Oscar Meunier, who spent some days in moulding that likeness, said that my features were more interesting than any he had modelled. He said that I presented a challenge to his skill, and that he had, in his own estimation, surpassed himself.'

'Did he now?' I said, in weighted tones.

Holmes flushed with annoyance. He *was* vain.

'Do you mean to say,' I continued, 'that you had to sit with that expression on your face for days on end? Did you offer yourself to this Monsieur Meunier, or was he so overcome by one glimpse of your interesting features that he cast himself at your feet and begged you to do him the honour — '

A cushion came sailing through the air towards me and I fended it off with my elbow.

'We struck up a mutually beneficial acquaintance,' said Holmes loftily. 'Monsieur Meunier is a most interesting and gifted man.'

He turned back to the mirror, in which he watched me, no doubt, as I recovered my dignity and donned a suitably sardonic expression.

'What will happen to your practice?' he asked, some days later.

'It will shrivel to nothing,' I murmured lazily. We were sitting on the bank of the river, watching the barges go by. Holmes sucked thoughtfully on his pipe.

'You don't sound very worried. Do you have enough money to live on?'

'Probably not.' I lit a cigarette. If I were not in mourning, I too would wear a straw hat, I thought, toying idly with the band of Holmes' headgear as it lay on the grass between us. I was all too well aware that even in Paris it was considered unconventional for one still in mourning to dine out and attend concerts as I had been doing. The hotel staff viewed my sudden change of mood since my arrival with some suspicion. But Mary — Mary would understand.

Her memory sobered me.

'I signed away all Mary's money and belongings, you know,' I said, 'to Mrs Forrester.'

Holmes' grey eyes widened. 'That was generous of you.'

'It was important,' I said. 'I could not bear to think of her feeling like — ' I saw him flinch, and trailed off. 'Anyway,' I said, 'I have a little.'

He gazed into the middle distance for a while, and then appeared to change the subject completely.

'I heard this morning,' he said, 'that Ralph Spencer is dead.'

I stared at him. So that was what this morning's excitement had been about. A telegram had arrived for him at the desk, just after breakfast, and he had gone out immediately on reading it, with no further explanation than that he would be back at the hotel for lunch. I had seen the old, familiar gleam in his eyes, and wisely had decided to refrain from questioning him.

'I went to the house,' he said. 'I took care not to be observed; but there was really no need for caution. There can be no doubt that it is true; relatives and mourners everywhere, and the news is already in the papers.'

'Good heavens, Holmes,' I said, clutching his hat in my excitement, 'this is wonderful! So now there is only Colonel Sebastian Moran.'

'Yes,' he said calmly. 'I will have to find some way of approaching my old contacts in London, so that I can keep myself informed of his movements. And we must watch the English papers,

Watson. I will get him.'

His eyes narrowed to bright slits in his face, and he drummed his fingers impatiently on his knee.

'And then,' I said softly, 'we will be able to go back home.'

'Back home. Yes.' Holmes' face relaxed, and again he stared pensively across the brown water.

'Watson,' he said slowly, after a pause, 'what if you sold your practice? Do you think you could get a good price for it?'

'Well — yes, I suppose I could,' I said, surprised. 'But — '

I left the question unasked. He spent a long time relighting his pipe. The eyes were hooded.

'Do you think — when the way is clear,' he said at last, 'and we can return to London, do you think you could move back in with me? To Baker Street?' He turned quickly to meet my gaze. 'I know it's only lodgings, and you are used to your own establishment, but — '

In a moment he would tell me that he earned so much a year, and that his prospects were good. I felt the laughter bubbling up inside me.

'Yes!' I said, as soon as I could, gasping for breath. 'Yes. All right. Yes!'

With a supreme effort, I suppressed my laughter, so as not to make a spectacle of myself to the approaching group of people taking their afternoon walk *en famille*: tall, distinguished-looking father, much younger mother in lace and parasole, boy, girl, nursemaid and baby, *tout comme il faut*.

'I accept,' I said soberly, when they had passed. Holmes regarded me with mischievous gravity.

'Thank you,' I added.

He nodded, and drew on his pipe.

# — POSTSCRIPT —

IT WAS, as Holmes had predicted, some months before an opportunity arose for us to move in on Colonel Sebastian Moran. The story of our subsequent investigation, leading to Moran's arrest for murder, is detailed in my 'Adventure of the Empty House'.

I had, of course, to preface it with an explanation of Holmes' 'return from the dead', and here, by combining the essential facts with a small measure of fiction, and by placing our meeting in London rather than in Paris, I flatter myself that I produced a fairly convincing story. At least, it appeared to convince the public at the time, although I am aware that it has come in for some discerning criticism since. My literary agent was of course well aware of my sojourn in Paris, and it was he who convinced me that it would be unwise and unnecessary to emphasise my reunion with Holmes by distinguishing it from his return to Baker Street.

We did return to Baker Street, however, as the reading public knows. I did sell my practice, to a distant relative of Holmes, in fact; though it was some time before I realised that Holmes himself had put up the money.

My friend was welcomed back to life with open arms by everyone outside the criminal fraternity, and I resumed my role as his Boswell. The next few years were, I think, the happiest of my life, in spite of the tragic and dangerous public events which occurred in the literary world a couple of years later, and cast a long shadow across the social and political landscape.

I leave here this account of the true circumstances surrounding Holmes' disappearance and return. Although I am well aware that from one point of view it can be seen as inadvisable and reckless of me to detail these events in writing, I felt that I owed it to myself to set down somewhere the real nature of the final problem, and the painful process of its resolution.